RUB IT IN

BY
KIRA SINCLAIR

First published in Great Britain 2012
by Mills & Boon, an imprint of Harlequin (UK) Limited,
Eton House, 18-24 Paradise Road, Richmond, Surrey TW9 1SR

© Kira Bazzel 2012

ISBN: 978 0 263 89734 0

30-0612

Harlequin (UK) policy is to use papers that are natural, renewable and recyclable products and made from wood grown in sustainable forests. The logging and manufacturing processes conform to the legal environmental regulations of the country of origin.

Printed and bound in Spain
by Blackprint CPI, Barcelona

really need a shower."

Simon's husky words tripped down Marcy's spine and she swallowed. Hard.

"Okay, but be quick about it. I have things to do," she said, just to remind them both where they stood.

Disappearing into the bathroom, his voice floated back out at her, "Like more dancing? I wouldn't mind sticking around to watch that show."

"No. No sticking, no show." Her face flushed hot.

"That's a shame. I could use some entertainment." He stuck his head back around the corner.

He was naked. At least what she could see of him. All wide shoulders and taut, tanned skin. The swell of well-defined pecs and just the hint of sculpted abs. A sprinkling of golden hair narrowed to a line down the center of his chest to disappear behind the dark wood of the door frame.

His heavy-lidded eyes searched her face, for what she wasn't sure. But whatever it was, he found it.

Simon wanted her.

And what Simon wanted, Simon got…

04753202

Dear Reader,

Have you ever read a book where a secondary character caught your attention and just wouldn't let it go? For me, that's what happened with hero and heroine, Simon and Marcy.

I knew the minute Marcy hit the page in *Bring It On,* she'd have her own story. She was feisty—the way I like my heroines—and therefore needed a really strong man. And, oh, Simon fit the bill. He is the epitome of "looks can be deceiving" and I fell a little in love with him myself. Please don't tell my husband.

My favorite relationships to write about are those where the characters strike sparks off each other the moment they meet. I don't mean arguing, although these two do plenty of that. But that combination of friction and attraction that you know is just a smoke screen hiding so much underneath. It's a lot of fun watching the haze clear.

I hope you enjoy reading Simon and Marcy's story! It was a pleasure to write. And be sure to check out *Bring It On* and *Take It Down*—the first two books in my ISLAND NIGHTS trilogy. You don't want to miss the fireworks leading up to *Rub It In.* I'd love to hear from you at kira@kirasinclair.com.

Best wishes,

Kira Sinclair

When not working as an office manager for a project management firm or juggling plot lines, **Kira Sinclair** spends her time on a small farm in north Alabama with her wonderful husband, two amazing daughters and a menagerie of animals. It's amazing to see how this self-proclaimed city girl has (or has not, depending on who you ask) adapted to country life. Kira enjoys hearing from her readers at her website, www.kirasinclair.com. Or stop by writingplayground. blogspot.com and join in the fight to stop the acquisition of an alpaca.

I'd like to dedicate this book to a group of women who have become sisters of my heart—Kimberly Lang, Andrea Laurence, Marilyn Puett and Danniele Worsham. Without you guys this journey wouldn't have happened—and it sure wouldn't have been as enjoyable even if it had. It seems like you've been a part of my life for as long as I can remember instead of only a few years. Y'all mean the world to me and I hope you guys know that. Love you!

1

"No, I can't wait until next week for the delivery. You promised it would arrive today," Marcy McKinney snarled into the phone. Taking a deep breath, she pasted a smile on her lips—because you really could hear it and her dad had always taught her you catch more flies with honey than vinegar—and said, "If you can't have the building supplies here by tomorrow then I want you to cancel my order and I'll get what I need somewhere else."

Slamming the phone back into its cradle would have felt good, but Marcy resisted. Barely. She had no idea where she'd find a store that could fill her rather large order, but she'd figure that out if the dissolute man on the other end of the phone actually called her bluff.

It wasn't as if hardware stores were thick on the ground in the middle of a secluded island in the Caribbean. Escape—the resort that she worked at as general manager—was actually the only thing on Île du Coeur. St. Lucia was the closest major hub, and it was forty-five minutes by ferry.

Getting the supplies from another island would

probably double the cost…but that wasn't her problem. It was Simon's.

She should probably feel bad about making Simon's life difficult. She didn't. It was his turn, damn it.

The resort would be closed for the next two weeks—their off-season hiatus. In two days she had a job interview for the general manager position at a boutique hotel in New York City. This could be her ticket off the island and back to civilization.

And nothing, not Simon or lost building supplies, defecting security personnel, not even—

"Marcy!"

—whatever was the latest disaster to hit her desk could keep her here.

Tina, the front desk clerk, bellowed down the back office hallway again.

"Coming," Marcy hollered back, modulating her voice to a pleasantly official tone. Scrambling out from behind her desk, she tried not to panic at the piles of paper, messages she still had to return and color-coded folders that needed her attention. She had so much to handle before she could walk out the door.

And by the time she could mark one thing off her list, three more tasks seemed to crop up to take its place.

The minute Marcy rounded the corner she knew there was trouble. Tina's normally brilliant smile was tight and as fake as her long red fingernails.

A couple, sunburned and cranky, stood on the opposite side of the counter.

"Mr. and Mrs. Smith." Tina rolled her eyes. While it wasn't their main focus, they had their share of Smiths, Joneses, Johnsons and any number of generically named guests who were most likely cheating on their spouses. Marcy didn't like it, but there was little she could do.

"Thank goodness. I've explained to—" the woman leaned forward and squinted at Tina's name tag "—Tina that we need to extend our stay." She held out her lobster-red arm, "As you can imagine, explaining how I received a second-degree sunburn while on a business trip to London might be slightly difficult." The woman sneered, including her companion in her raking gaze.

"And as I've told Mrs. Smith…" This time Tina couldn't help but emphasize the misnomer. Marcy probably should scold her, but she wouldn't. "We have no available rooms, as the resort is closing for two weeks tomorrow."

"We'll pay whatever."

Marcy's own smile was tight as she said, "It isn't a matter of money, ma'am." She refused to let the false name pass her lips. "The resort is undergoing construction and our insurance company won't allow any guests on the premises for liability reasons."

The woman's scowl deepened. Marcy could see the snit she was about to unleash as it built in the back of her beautiful green eyes. Cutting it off at the pass, Marcy continued, "However, I'd be happy to contact a resort on St. Lucia and see if something is available while you recover."

Instead of a tirade, a sigh of relief exited through the woman's pink and pouty lips. "Oh, yes, that would be wonderful. If you wouldn't mind." Marcy fought the urge to smack the smile off *Mrs. Smith's* face.

"Give us a minute." She ground out the words through clenched teeth as she pulled Tina into the back office behind her. "Run down the list of resorts on the island and see what you can find. Start with the family-oriented resorts. The more obnoxious the kids, the better."

Tina giggled. "Happy to."

Marcy left her to it, heading back to her desk and the pile of work waiting for her there. Despite it being afternoon, the other offices were already dark. Most of the staff were busy packing their own bags for a change. Everyone except a skeleton crew left the island for these two weeks each year. When a tropical paradise was your home, vacations usually meant visiting family you hadn't seen in forever.

Marcy had no family to see. Her mother had died when she was a little girl. Her father, a hotel manager himself, had died five years ago. She had no brothers or sisters, and only one aunt on her father's side, but the last time she'd heard from Suellen had been at her father's funeral.

She had several close friends from college, but they were all scattered around the country. And while she talked to them as often as possible, most of them were busy starting families and building careers. Several years ago they'd given up trying to plan a girls' week away. It was just too hard to work around all their schedules.

Some of the staff would stay. She'd spent last year here herself. In theory having the entire resort to yourself—including all the amenities the guests used but she never had time for—wasn't a bad thing. If she'd actually taken time to use those amenities. Instead, she'd spent the entire two weeks—weeks that were supposed to be her vacation—working.

Not this year. Tomorrow afternoon she was leaving. Marcy sighed. Two blissful weeks with no Simon—the bane of her existence.

In her opinion, no laid-back surf god should ever own a resort. It had gotten to the point where just the sight of Simon's low-riding shorts and tight T-shirts had begun to grate on her nerves. They were running a business!

Besides, no man should look that sexy while somehow still managing to appear as if donning clothing had been an afterthought. The problem with that kind of…demeanor was that most of the time she feared Simon was two steps away from shedding his clothes again just because they were annoying him. And she didn't want that. Really, she didn't. It would set a bad example for the employees.

She preferred men with more structured wardrobes. The kind who wore business suits every day…and liked it. If she discovered Simon owned a single pair of tailored pants or a silk tie—let alone a suit—she'd die of shock.

Before moving to the island she'd lived in cities. Lots of them. London, Prague, Chicago, San Francisco. And she'd loved them all. But her heart belonged to New York, where the men definitely knew how to wear their suits. And run their businesses.

Simon might have had the money to purchase the resort, but he didn't seem to care much about keeping it going. Even the disheveled blond hair that notoriously hung in his dark blue eyes bothered her. She constantly wanted to sweep it out of the way, but the one time she'd given in to the impulse her hand had tingled for twenty minutes. And that was the last thing she needed.

But it was difficult, as a woman, not to recognize that Simon was an attractive man. He was tall, his athletic body moving with a grace that seemed counterintuitive considering his height. Charm and devilment mixed with his inherent sex appeal—a potentially lethal combination.

But she refused to feel attracted. Not to her boss. She'd learned her lesson the first time around that block.

"Marcy." The two-way radio on her hip squawked. "We have a problem."

Tom, their only remaining security person, thought everything was a problem. Since the head of security, Zane Edwards, had left to follow the woman he loved to Atlanta and his replacement had lasted all of six weeks, Tom was all she had right now. Marcy couldn't really blame the guy for his "the sky is falling" attitude—he was so far out of his element. Tom was great at watching the monitors and keeping drunken guests in line. But at twenty-two, he was hardly ready to take on the task of head of security for a resort as large as Escape.

Marcy was hoping to fix that problem before she left, as well. On her desk sat three résumés from three very capable candidates. All were to arrive on the afternoon ferry. They'd stay the night, be interviewed tomorrow, tour the facility and then leave on the morning ferry. Simon had balked at the expense, but after Zane's replacement hadn't been able to handle island life, she wasn't making that mistake again.

The last stragglers would join them. Marcy was half packed and come hell or high water would be on the last ferry.

Snatching the radio off her belt, Marcy huffed, "What is it, Tom?"

"Several men—" she could hear the hesitation in his

voice "—just got off the ferry. You said not to allow anyone off."

What she'd said was not to allow any guests off. She had no doubt, based on the falter in his voice, that the group he was referring to were her construction workers.

"Do the men have toolboxes, ladders or anything else resembling construction equipment, by any chance?"

"Yes." He sounded surprised, and Marcy fought hard not to roll her eyes.

"Could they be the crew coming to handle the maintenance and renovations while we're closed?" she asked patiently.

"Maybe." He drew out the single word, telling her that he was quickly reevaluating the situation in front of him. Really, he was a good boy who could do with just a little more common sense and practical life experience. Marcy could hear a rustle as he placed his hand over the phone. Unfortunately it didn't dampen the sound enough for her to miss as he asked the men, "Are you construction guys?"

Their yes was muffled but audible nonetheless.

"Uh, yeah, they are."

"Great. Maybe next time you'll ask them why they're here first before calling me up with a non-crisis. Put them in the old bunkhouse."

The bunkhouse was left over from the days when the island had been a cocoa plantation, though it had been updated and renovated since then. The building was rarely used, but it would serve perfectly for the next two weeks. Most of the permanent employees had either bungalows at the back of the property, like hers, or living quarters close to the job, like their chef, who had a rather large apartment above the kitchens.

Great, now she had workers but no supplies for them to actually do anything.

Blowing at a wisp of hair that had fallen into her eyes, Marcy flopped back into the executive chair behind her desk, not sure whether she wanted to scream, cry or start smashing things. Probably a little of all three.

Her to-do list was a mile long. Nothing was going right.

And she had no doubt that the minute Simon realized she was leaving tomorrow he would blow a gasket. Not that her departure should surprise him, since she'd told him in person, sent him an email and reminded him a dozen times over the past few weeks.

However, if there was one thing she'd learned about Simon Reeves, it was that his brain was like Swiss cheese and his hearing was more than selective…as in nonexistent.

But that was another thing that was his problem, not hers.

Pulling up the document she'd been working on, Marcy looked at the detailed instructions she'd written in an effort to help Simon through the next two weeks—and if the interview went well, to help her replacement. Part of her had wanted to leave him with nothing, but that just wasn't her style. She'd put too much time and effort into the resort to see Simon ruin it the minute she walked out the door.

The document was currently sitting at twenty-two pages. Marcy was a little worried the sheer size of the thing would prevent Simon from reading it.

She stared at it for several seconds. *Cut it down, or*

leave it as is? It was an argument she'd had multiple times over the past few days. Ultimately she came to the same conclusion she'd come to numerous times. Once again, what Simon chose to do or not do was not her problem.

And hopefully, if things went according to plan, wouldn't ever be again.

SIMON FOUGHT THE URGE to grab the first thing and throw it at the door when a loud knock blasted through his office. The scene he was writing wasn't working and he couldn't figure out why. Frustration rode him hard and probably wasn't helping the situation. Neither was the bustling noise that even here, behind the closed door of his private office, couldn't be disguised.

The staff was happy at the prospect of having two weeks off. Frankly, he was happy to see them leave, at least for a little while. Having the place virtually to himself was going to be a godsend.

He was months behind on the deadline for his current manuscript. It was so bad that he'd actually unplugged his phone and uninstalled the mail program from his computer to avoid email from his editor and agent. If he didn't finish this thing in the next two weeks he could probably kiss his career goodbye. Again.

Thanks to Courtney's betrayal three years ago, the resulting plagiarism scandal and his fruitless attempts to prove the work was really his, his career had already dangled by a thread once. He really didn't want to go through that again.

Île du Coeur and Escape were supposed to have provided him the space and seclusion to rebuild his career. Instead, they'd both become a huge time-suck.

Buying the place had seemed like a brilliant idea. He had the capital to purchase the island, and the resort would provide the necessary revenue stream for upkeep. A manager should have taken the responsibilities off his shoulders, leaving him free to lock himself inside his office to write.

Should have. Somehow things hadn't exactly gone the way he'd hoped.

The problem was that not a soul on the island—not even Marcy—knew who he was. And he liked it that way. It protected his work. He wrote under a pseudonym and always had.

He'd wanted a clean break from the life he'd left behind. Wanted to start again and pretend the entire affair had never happened. Unfortunately, it was difficult to forget being betrayed by someone you loved.

That sort of deception tended to color your opinion of people. Always making you wonder who was going to stab you in the back next.

"Simon!" Marcy's voice exploded through the wood of the door along with the rattling of the knob that he'd locked for just such an occasion.

Knowing from experience that she wouldn't leave until he listened to her, Simon minimized his documents, brought up a gaming program he used to make everyone think he was just wasting time in here, and walked across the room. Yanking open the door, he lounged inside the jamb, one arm stretched across the gaping area so that she'd either have to stay on her side of the door or duck underneath his arm. She wouldn't do that. One good thing about Marcy—she avoided coming into contact with him at all costs.

In the beginning he'd been happy. The last thing he had time for was a romantic complication with his manager. She was there to work and make his life easier, and from his experience, mixing business with pleasure rarely made anything easier. But the more she avoided him, the more he became aware of her deliberate distance. A distance that made him want to ruffle her feathers by pushing against the boundaries she'd erected. It was pointless, but he couldn't help it.

Even now he inched his body closer to hers, crowding into her personal space just to see her spine stiffen. The infinitesimal shuffle backward was rewarding, especially when she stopped it midway, consciously determined not to let him fluster her.

A grin tugged at the corners of his lips but he wouldn't let it grab hold. Instead, he asked, "What do you need?"

She raised her hand, a sheaf of papers fluttering with the force of the motion. "*We* need to go over everything before I leave tomorrow. I sent you an appointment by email."

"I uninstalled the program."

Her eyes widened before narrowing to glittering slits. He loved it when Marcy got mad. Her blue eyes sparkled with a passion that made the muscles in his stomach tighten. She reminded him of a pixie; in fact, he almost hadn't hired her because she looked as if a good stiff breeze could knock her on her ass. But beneath that tiny frame was a spine of steel and the heart of a drill sergeant. She was good at what she did, if a little too organized and into unimportant details for his liking.

"Why would you do something stupid like that?"

Simon shrugged, not caring that she'd just called him stupid. It was by far the least offensive term she'd used for him in the past two years.

"Because I'm avoiding someone."

"Well, you can't avoid me."

If that wasn't the most obvious statement of the year he didn't know what was. He chose to let the softball setup she'd just given him slide by.

"What do you mean before you leave? Did I know you were going to be gone tomorrow? Isn't the construction crew supposed to be starting? You can't leave until you're sure they know what they're doing. I don't have time to deal with them, even for a day."

Marcy shook her head slowly, the slick blond strands of her ever-present ponytail whipping behind her. He watched the rise and fall of her chest as she took a deep breath, held it and finally let it go. As chests went, hers was…fine. He tended to prefer big-breasted women with a huge handful he could grab hold of. Although it was hard to tell where Marcy was concerned. Despite the fact that they worked in a tropical location and the dress code was fairly relaxed, she insisted on wearing business suits when she was working—which was always.

He'd decided that the slacks, skirts, blouses and tailored jackets that still somehow seemed a little too roomy over her body were her personal armor. He just hadn't been able to discover what she was hiding from. At first he'd wondered if it was men in general. He worried maybe she'd been attacked. But as he'd watched her dealing, smiling and, hell, almost flirting with their male guests over the years he'd decided that couldn't possibly be it.

And while she hadn't taken a lover in the past two years—at least not one that he was aware of, and he knew everything that happened on his island— it wasn't for lack of offers. If she hadn't said yes to anyone, it was because she hadn't wanted to. Marcy McKinney was definitely the captain of her destiny and knew exactly what she wanted at all times.

It exhausted him just to think about that kind of structured existence.

"I'm not leaving for the day."

"But you just said you were."

"No, I said I needed to go over this—" she waved the papers again; now that he looked at them, the stack appeared rather large…and the type on them awfully small "—before I leave tomorrow. I'm taking two weeks' vacation."

"The hell you say."

"We talked about this, Simon." He heard her warning tone, but chose to ignore it.

"I don't remember you mentioning you were leaving *these* two weeks." Although it was possible he hadn't been paying attention to her. He did have a habit of tuning Marcy out when she spoke. But it was usually because whatever she was saying wasn't important to him—at least not more important than the other thoughts flowing through his mind.

He'd learned early that pretending to listen and nodding appropriately were usually enough to keep her satisfied. That way, they both walked away with a smile. Win, win.

"I most certainly did. We talked. I sent you reminders. Hell, I even went on your computer and blocked the days out on your calendar."

"You went on my computer?" A nasty mix of anger, disappointment and betrayal burst through him. It was a knee-jerk reaction, the result of what Courtney had done. Not only had she stolen his work, she'd destroyed every speck of evidence that it had ever existed on his computer. She'd ruined his backup hard drive. She'd left him nothing to fight with.

He didn't like people messing with his computer.

Clenching his hands into fists, Simon invaded Marcy's space, bringing them nose-to-nose. She sucked a hard breath through her teeth, but didn't back away. Her bright blue eyes searched his, puzzled and off-kilter. It should have been enough for him, but it wasn't.

"Why did you do that?"

"Jesus, Simon, what is wrong with you?" She finally pushed against him, trying to get him out of her personal space. He didn't move. "I knew you'd ignore my emails and forget our conversation. I was trying to help."

"I didn't ask for your help," he growled at her.

Her eyes flared, the surprise quickly being overwhelmed by irritation. "Actually, you did when you hired me," she snapped.

For the first time Simon realized he was towering above her, his tall body curled over hers. Anyone else probably would have bowed backward under the intimidation tactic. Not Marcy. Sometimes it was easy to forget how tiny she was. Her confidence and competence more than made up for her size.

"Move back," she said and then waited patiently for him to do exactly what she'd ordered. Everyone always seemed to fall in line for Marcy. It was irritating.

Just once he wished she'd do him a favor and fall in line for *him*.

Instead, he slowly stepped away. She glared at him, her eyes sharp and hurt. He refused to apologize or explain his reaction.

And yet somehow the words fell from his lips anyway. "Look, I'm sorry, Marcy. I need you here during the break. I have something important that requires all my attention. I don't have time to handle the resort, too."

"Bullshit."

His molars clanked together. "Excuse me?"

"Only a few of the staff will be left. I'm interviewing the candidates for head of security tomorrow before I leave. The construction crew is here, their materials will be tomorrow. Before I leave, I'll make sure they have a clear agenda for the two weeks. These—" she waved the damn papers again "—contain every possible scenario that could come up and how to handle it. It's the perfect time for me to take a vacation. You can't afford for me to be gone while the resort is full."

She had a point there. Although in a couple weeks he should be done with this book and could probably handle things for a little while.

"I promise I'll make it up to you," he said, flashing her one of his patented grins in the hope that it might soften her up a little. It had always worked on women in the past, although somehow Marcy seemed immune. "Next month you can take as much time off as you want." Within reason, but they'd cross that bridge only when she forced him to the edge of it.

"No, Simon. You can't charm your way into getting what you want with me. I have plans."

"Change them."

"Nonrefundable travel plans."

"I'll pay the difference."

"And people waiting on me to show up. Simon, I'm leaving tomorrow afternoon. Short of you kidnapping me—and not even you are that stupid—you're going to have to find a way to deal without me for the next two weeks."

His hands clenched again and a headache began to pound behind his eyes. She didn't understand and he couldn't explain it to her, not without revealing his secret. Or telling her why his privacy was so important to him that he would hide his identity in the first place. And he just wasn't willing to make himself that vulnerable, not even with Marcy.

She was leaving, huh? Well, they'd just have to see about that.

2

THE RESORT WAS QUIET. Disturbingly silent without guests. There was no one splashing or yelling at the pool as she dragged her three matching pieces of luggage behind her. No couples strolling hand-in-hand across the warm sand. No painted-up thirtysomethings in string bikinis sipping drinks beneath cabanas and waiting to pick up whatever hot guy strolled past.

She was used to the hustle and bustle, and the place seemed almost eerie without it. As if the island itself were sad that no one was there to play and frolic.

The locals had a legend about Île du Coeur, something about finding your heart's desire—whether it was what you'd come looking for or not. She'd never really paid that much attention to it because she didn't believe in that sort of stuff, but at this moment the island felt almost alive.

As if maybe anything was possible.

The caws and whistles of the birds deep in the jungle and the ringing of hammers as the work crew repaired the restaurant roof broke through the moment. Their supplies had arrived on the morning ferry, and the last of the staff and the two candidates she hadn't hired for head of security had left. She'd been surprised when Xavier, the man she'd hired, said he was prepared to stay and start immediately. She wondered briefly what kind of person could pack their entire life into a single suitcase, but decided she didn't have time to find out. He was more than qualified for the position.

The repair of the roof was the first in a long list of upgrades and maintenance the crew would be handling over the next two weeks. Hurricane season was upon them and the last thing they needed was leaky roofs or unstable buildings. Marcy seriously hoped for their sake that everything went smoothly. She'd never actually seen Simon lose his temper, but something told her that between the distraction, the length of the list she'd left and her departure, he was precariously close to the deep end.

Too bad.

Served him right for not appreciating the long hours, detailed work and effort she'd put into this place for him. Instead of praise, she got snarky remarks and needling innuendos. Instead of understanding, she got exasperation and a locked door in her face.

Hopefully, no more. She was going to charm the socks off whomever she had to in order to get the hell off this island and back to the big city. Cramped apartments, twenty-four-hour Chinese food, men in suits, museums, shows, culture…that was her idea of paradise.

Her suitcases bumped across the raised boards of the dock. Normally she was a light traveler, preferring to fit as much as possible into one carry-on bag. The thought of losing all her luggage made her chest ache. But during her time at Escape, she'd collected more stuff than she'd realized. And hoping that she'd be able to tender her resignation from New York, she'd packed everything she owned. Well, at least anything she'd wanted to take with her. Her father had taught her that some things just weren't worth the trouble.

Arranging her luggage in descending order, Marcy lined them up perpendicular to the boards, stared out across the vacant water and then looked at her watch. She was a little early. With a shrug, she plopped her butt onto the top of her largest suitcase and prepared to wait. She thought about pulling out the novel she'd packed into her carry-on but decided it wasn't worth the effort. She had ten, fifteen minutes at the most.

But, oh, it called to her. She couldn't remember the last time she'd been able to crack open the spine of a good thriller. She loved them, a holdover from the days when her father would pass along his finished books to her. They'd shared that excitement, spending hours discussing the finer points of their favorite books over dinner.

Her love of thrillers wasn't the only thing she'd inherited from her dad. His workaholic, detail-oriented, high-expectation requirements had also come with the genes. A familiar sadness crept up on her. He'd been gone for almost five years, but it still hadn't gotten any easier.

Although she supposed there was a silver lining. He'd have been so disappointed in her over the New York debacle. Tears stung her eyes, but Marcy refused to let them fall. It had been two and a half years, and still it upset her.

She'd been so lonely. Looking for companionship and support and someone to share her life with. Marcy thought she'd found that in Christoph Fischer. Yes, she knew better than to sleep with someone she worked with—her boss, no less. But he'd swept her off her feet and she'd been helpless to resist. It didn't help that they'd spent so much time together at work.

Even before she'd started at his hotel, she'd heard rumors that he and his wife were divorcing. A year later, when he began asking her out, she assumed the divorce was final. Shame on her for not checking!

The humiliation of discovering—in the middle of a crowded ballroom filled with industry professionals—that his wife was very much still a part of his life was something she'd never forget. Neither was having champagne thrown in her face and obscenities rained down over her head. Marcy had never thought of herself as a home wrecker, had never wanted or planned to be one.

Being lied to by someone she'd trusted was terrible enough, but then he'd had the audacity to fire her. And blackball her with every other reputable hotel in the city...

She'd taken the first job that she could—Simon's offer—as far away from the city as she could get. She'd needed the time away. She'd desperately needed the job. And she'd needed the line on her résumé—a buffer between the debacle and whatever would come next.

But that was all behind her now. And this interview was the opportunity to make a fresh start. Surely, over two years later, everyone would have moved on to juicier gossip. She'd gotten the interview after all.

This job was her ticket back home. Back to civilization and structure.

A frown on her face, Marcy looked at her watch again. The tropical sun was baking her scalp and exposed legs. If she'd known she was going to sit here for a half hour she would have put on sunscreen. The ferry was definitely late. Standing, she walked to the edge of the dock and craned her neck to see if the squat vessel was visible across the water. It wasn't.

This was exactly the kind of thing that drove her crazy! The entire place ran on island time and she was so sick and tired of it. Didn't anyone respect punctuality anymore? The ferry was routinely late. People waited five, ten, even fifteen minutes on occasion, but never this long.

Maybe the ferry crew figured that with a skeleton staff and no guests to deliver, there was no hurry. With a scowl, Marcy returned to perch on top of her bag. They were going to get an earful from her whenever they did finally arrive. She had a plane to catch. Thank God she'd built some "disaster" time into her schedule.

SIMON STARED out the window at Marcy. He'd left his apartments and walked around to the far side of the building so he could watch her. Part of him couldn't help but chuckle at the agitated way she kept jumping up from her seat on that coral-colored suitcase to pace along the length of the dock, only to sit back down again.

The suitcase was unexpected—he would have thought she was more of a traditional black or brown kinda girl—but her reaction wasn't. The only reason Simon was standing there watching her was that he was a coward.

He'd meant to go down there at three, to cut her off as she reached the dock and explain that she wasn't going anywhere because he'd called and canceled the ferry service for the next two weeks. But he'd gotten involved in a scene. The words had flowed, and considering that hadn't happened in the past few days, he'd been reluctant to walk away.

And now he was going to pay the price. No doubt a tongue-lashing was in his future. Was it wrong that he sort of enjoyed riling Marcy up?

When she was angry her blue eyes flashed, reminding him of sapphires turned to catch the light. Her skin tinted a pale pink color and her jaw tightened so hard that he wanted to kiss her senseless just to startle her into letting go.

But he wouldn't allow himself to go there. She was too valuable as his manager. He had a policy of never seducing employees. And he had no desire for a relationship. He'd never been great at them before Courtney. And after, the idea of trusting someone that much again didn't sit well with him.

Marcy spun on her heel, knocking the smallest of her suitcases over and starting a domino effect that ended with all her luggage hitting the dock. He couldn't hear the bang from behind the protection of the glass, but he could imagine that it—and her growl of frustration—had been loud.

Logically, he realized the longer he waited the worse the explosion was going to be.

Taking a deep breath, he schooled his features into a mask of indifference and headed out into the afternoon heat.

Tucking his hands into the pockets of his khaki shorts, Simon ambled toward the dock. He broke through the line of rich tropical foliage to find Marcy had righted her bags and was staring in his direction, no doubt having heard his feet on the path.

"Simon," she said, her face twisted into a frown already. Not great. "What are you doing?"

Propping his hip against the wooden railing that surrounded the dock, he said, "I came to tell you that the ferry isn't coming."

"What?" she exclaimed. The already high color on her cheeks flamed even brighter. She looked behind her over the water, as if the ferry might turn a corner and prove him a liar at any moment. "The ferry comes every day. Twice."

"Not today."

"What happened? Was there an accident? Is anyone injured?"

Simon felt the pinch of guilt as he realized that her first assumption was only an accident could stop the one form of transportation on and off the island. And she was worried about other people more than her own inconvenience.

He had to come clean.

"No, no accident. I called and canceled the service."

Marcy swung her eyes back to him. They were wide with confusion. The cloud of her long blond hair, usually pulled tight into a smooth ponytail during work hours, floated around her face. He liked it down and couldn't remember a single time in the past two years that he'd seen it this way. Free. Not exactly a word he would have normally used to describe Marcy. His gaze traveled down her body and he realized she wasn't wearing her trademark suit, either. Instead she wore a pale green polo—every button done up to her throat—and a pair of crisp khaki shorts. Had he ever seen her legs bare?

Shaking his head, he jerked his mind back to where it should be. "Why the hell would you do that?"

He shrugged, knowing the inevitable shitstorm he was about to release. "Because I couldn't let you leave. I need you here, Marcy, and I'll do whatever it takes to keep you here for the next two weeks."

"You…you…" she sputtered, her eyes turning hard and sharp. "You canceled the ferry?"

"Yep." While he tried to maintain the relaxed air he'd adopted the minute he set foot on the tropical island, his eyes stayed clear and focused on Marcy. He honestly had no idea what she might do. "You gave me the idea."

"What are you talking about?"

"You're the one who suggested I kidnap you. I always try to take your advice."

She growled low in the back of her throat. It was the same sort of sound the pit bull he'd had as a child used to make when a stranger entered their yard. A warning. Only this time he couldn't shake the feeling that he was the one about to have his hand bitten.

"You do no such thing. Ignoring me has become a sort of hobby for you and we both know it."

Well, he had, but until this moment he hadn't realized she'd been aware.

"Fine," she said, her jaw hard and tight. "I'll call Rusty for a private launch."

He debated whether or not to let her make the call. He knew what Rusty's answer would be—his and that of every other private boating service on this side of St. Lucia. He'd called them all and promised to pull the resort's business from them if they accepted Marcy's request.

And where that kind of threat hadn't worked, he'd used bribery instead, offering to pay for their refusal to provide service to the island for the next two weeks.

Details were his thing, and he wasn't about to bend over backward to keep Marcy on the island only to let her get away through other means. He'd closed off every possible avenue of escape.

Marcy's phone was halfway to her ear when he decided it might be better for him if he cut her off at the pass. Perhaps hearing it from him instead of Rusty would lessen the impact…and her anger.

"I wouldn't bother. I think you'll find everyone is booked."

Her phone dangled from her loose fingers as she stared at him. "What do you mean?"

"Just that I've paid them more not to come than you could pay them to come."

And it had been worth every frickin' penny.

She raked him with prickly blue eyes, making him feel as if ice was melting down his spine. She really did know how to use that gaze to intimidate. But he was a master himself, so it just wouldn't work.

"You have no respect for anyone but yourself, do you?" she asked in a low voice that scared him even more than if she'd started yelling.

Time for the platitudes.

"Look, I'll make it up to you. Name your price. A raise? An all-expenses-paid vacation? Diamonds? What will it cost me to keep you here for the next two weeks?"

"Not everything is for sale, Simon. Do I look like I care about diamonds?"

He couldn't help it—his eyes traveled down Marcy's body, from the tip of her blond head to the pale pink toenails that peeked out from her sandals. Really, she'd almost begged him to. And he had to admit that she didn't look like the kind of woman who cared about jewels.

Oh, Marcy was stylish in a put-together business-woman sort of way. But she didn't drape herself in jewelry like some of the women he'd been known to associate with. In fact, the only jewelry she wore was a pair of small diamond studs and a single gold ring that looked suspiciously like a wedding band, only it was on her right hand.

"I had plans. Important plans. You can't manipulate everyone and everything to get your way, Simon. You are not God and no one gave you the right to meddle in my life."

His own anger was starting to kindle deep in his belly. He needed her here, damn it.

"I'm your boss, Marcy. I said I need you here. That should have been the end of the discussion. You're valuable to me. Any other boss would have given you an ultimatum."

"Right. Instead, you canceled the ferry and didn't give me any choice in the matter."

"Everyone has a choice."

Her eyes sharpened before narrowing to tiny slits that reminded him of the arrow slots he'd seen in medieval castles—deadly depending on what lay behind.

"You know what—you're right. I do have a choice. You can keep me prisoner here, Simon, but you can't make me work. You can't force me to lift a finger."

"I'll fire you."

She threw her arms up in the air, letting them fall back down, the motion disturbing the cloud of hair around her face. The laugh that accompanied the motion was far from humorous. "Go ahead. I'm tired of busting my ass for you. I'm tired of going above and beyond to make this place run smoothly, be successful and high quality. I'm tired of having to fight you every step of the way when I try to do the job you hired me for."

"Sounds like you just need a nap."

"No, what I need is a vacation, part of the reason I was leaving for two weeks."

"Only part?"

Marcy tipped her head sideways and studied him for several seconds before answering. "Yep, part. I also had a job interview in New York in two days."

Simon didn't understand. Sure, he needled her on a regular basis—it was fun to watch the steam pour out of her ears. And he often questioned her tactics and thought she bothered him with details that he didn't give a damn about.

But she worked in paradise.

"Why the hell would you want to leave here—" he threw his arms wide to indicate the beach, jungle and gleaming water that surrounded them "—for the rat race of New York? Here you have a perpetual vacation outside your door."

"One I don't ever get to take because I'm too damned busy taking care of everyone else. Just once I'd like to sit in one of those lounge chairs on the beach and sip a fruity drink and think frothy thoughts. Or get a massage."

Her eyes turned wistful for the barest moment, but he caught it before it disappeared. He'd never realized she hadn't used Tiffany's services. God, she had the most amazing hands.

Shaking his head, Simon realized he needed to keep focused on the little spitfire in front of him or risk getting singed.

"Please," he scoffed. They both knew Marcy wouldn't last fifteen minutes in that lounge chair before her body would start twitching with the need to do something. "You could have done that any time you wanted. You make me sound like a slave driver. I didn't ask you to come into the office at five o'clock every morning. Or work until seven at night. You did that all on your own."

"Because someone had to do it."

Had he really been that blind? He didn't think so. He might have his nose stuck in the Word program on his computer, but he did pay attention to what was happening around him. It was just that his idea of what was important and Marcy's seemed to be diametrically opposed. Had she needed help at some point and he hadn't realized it?

"Do you need an assistant? Is that it?"

"No, that's not it," she exclaimed, frustration pulling down the corners of her mouth. "You don't get it, Simon, and I don't think you ever will. All I wanted was for you to give a damn about this place."

"I do!" he shouted.

"Not from where I'm sitting. New York is home and I want to go back. It's where I came from and where I belong. Working here is frustrating and I can't take it anymore."

"Bullshit. You belong here. You're wonderful at your job." Hadn't he said that over and over again? Hell, he'd basically kidnapped her because he couldn't survive two weeks without her. Wasn't that demonstration enough?

"Nice to know you realize it."

"Of course I do."

Shaking her head, Marcy gathered her bags and pushed past him up the path.

"Where are you going?"

"To see if there's another way off this island."

A churning sensation started deep in his belly and quickly swirled out to overwhelm him. He knew there wasn't—he'd made sure of that—but that didn't seem to stop the nerves. Marcy couldn't leave, not today, not ever. As if he didn't already have enough reasons for keeping her here, knowing she wanted to interview for a position that would take her away permanently only made him more determined.

Over his dead body.

"There isn't. I even called the tourist helicopter services. I've covered all the bases."

Marcy whirled to face him again, framed by the thick foliage that surrounded the path. The vibrant green only seemed to emphasize the blue of her eyes, the pale blond of her hair and the deep tan of her long legs. Her fist gripped the handles of her luggage, the knuckles turning white with the force of her hold and the exertion of her control over her own temper.

Was he perverse to want to see what she'd do if she really let that temper fly? Oh, he knew she had it, but he also realized he'd never once seen the full brunt of it. He'd often thought passionate women made the best lovers because they rarely held back in life or in bed.

Marcy was the exception to that rule. He had no doubt there was passion beneath the controlled, tight, competent facade that she showed the world, despite the fact that he'd never seen it.

"Don't think you've won, Simon."

A smile twitched at the corners of his lips. From where he stood that was exactly what had happened,

Marcy couldn't leave the island and they both knew it. He also knew that despite what she might say, she was enough of a workaholic that she couldn't sit idly by and do nothing while there were things to be handled.

He was counting on her innate tendencies to override any residual anger that might still linger by tomorrow. He figured she'd stew today for sure. Tomorrow morning, bright and early, she'd be back in her office.

She just couldn't help it.

3

WHIRRING, BANGING and the loud *pa-pow* of a nail gun reverberated through Simon's skull. The construction crew had begun their noise at seven o'clock this morning. Three hours later it was getting worse, not better.

Normally, waking up that early wouldn't have bothered him—he rarely slept past five anyway—but last night he'd stayed up until 2:00 a.m. reading through a stubborn scene.

He was bleary-eyed, tired and cranky. Not to mention that the mother of all headaches pounded relentlessly behind his eyes.

After a rather loud clamor that he could only assume meant someone had dropped an entire load of metal onto a hard surface, Simon jumped out of his chair and yelled, "Enough!" Not that they could hear him.

Surely they could work somewhere else on the island for a while and give him a break. A nap, that was all he needed to get back into the groove he'd found the other day. The fact that his mind kept returning to his conversation with Marcy when it should have been concentrating on the story in front of him had nothing to do with his foul mood.

Rubbing his hands over his face, trying to clear his cloudy vision, Simon headed for Marcy's office.

Halfway down the hallway, Xavier, the new head of security Marcy had hired yesterday, walked out of the elevator.

"Oh, good," he said, stepping back onto the car and holding open the door so Simon could join him. "I was just coming to see you. I'd like to sit down and discuss the existing security measures and evaluate any improvements I'd like to make."

With a sigh, Simon closed his eyes for a moment before answering, "Our previous head of security was former CIA. Trust me when I say I can't think of a single change you'd want or need to make. Zane was meticulous."

"As am I," Xavier answered with a smile on his lips but a hard glint in his dark brown eyes. "I'd still like to meet with you. Start out on the right foot, so to speak."

"I'm pretty busy for the next few weeks. Can this wait until later?"

"Marcy mentioned the resort was closed and that a construction crew had been hired. I assume it would be more cost-effective to handle any adjustments while the crew is already here instead of having to bring them back."

The throb that had set up residence behind Simon's eyes increased in intensity. He realized Xavier had a valid point, but he really, really didn't have the time or energy to deal with this right now. Saving money wasn't always the most important objective. Something Marcy had a difficult time understanding.

It appeared that Xavier might reside in that camp, as well. Maybe putting them together was a good idea.

The elevator dinged their arrival on the lowest floor. The doors slid open silently and Simon reached to hold them back.

"I'm heading to Marcy's office right now. Why don't you follow me and discuss this with her?"

Xavier entered the long hallway, glancing back over his shoulder. "I would, but she said she no longer works here and that I'd need to deal directly with you."

Simon stopped in his tracks. "What did you say?"

"Marcy said I should deal directly with you."

"No, before that."

"Marcy said she quit or you fired her. Or maybe it was both? I didn't quite understand why she was still on the island, but I didn't figure it was my business to ask."

Simon knew exactly why she was still here. Because he wouldn't let her leave. But he hadn't thought she was serious about quitting. His threat of firing her had been a bluff. She'd known it, right? Why would he fire her and then continue to keep her prisoner here? It sort of defeated the purpose.

"Crap!" The single word exploded from Simon's mouth.

Pushing past Xavier, he headed for the offices at a sprint.

"She isn't there."

Even before Simon skidded around the corner he knew Xavier was right and the office would be vacant. First, no light shone from the small space. Second, there was no noise. Every other time he'd ventured into Marcy's territory—and he admitted exhausting all other options before giving in to that last resort—there

Rub It In

was a flurry of activity. Phones ringing, keys being rhythmically tapped, printers whirring. Today there was nothing. The only sounds were from the construction crew outside.

A huge knot of dread tightened in the pit of his stomach. What had he done?

Backing out of her empty office, he almost barreled into Xavier, who was waiting in the hallway, his rather large arms crossed over his chest.

"Where is she?" he asked.

Xavier shrugged. "The last time I saw her she was by the pool."

With a few strides Simon crossed the lobby and headed out the front door, Xavier a few steps behind him.

"Look, we'll talk later. After I've straightened this out. In the meantime, why don't you go unpack or something?" The man had just moved his entire life to their tiny island. Didn't he have something better to do?

Raising his hands, Xavier backed away slowly. "I've already unpacked, but I suppose I can find something else to pass the time."

Bright sunlight blinded Simon, spearing straight into his already gritty eyes and making him wish he'd stopped long enough to pick up his sunglasses. And some aspirin.

The construction noise was even louder without the barrier of walls to muffle it. It almost made him want to look at the six-foot-long list Marcy had plopped onto his desk, to figure out what the hell the crew could be working on. But that was the first step down a slippery slope. Looking at the list would lead to having an opinion about what they were doing, which would lead to getting involved and the entire project would become a distraction he didn't need.

It wasn't that he didn't care what went on around the resort, but he couldn't afford to take time away from his writing. Not if he wanted to keep his career from completely tanking.

By the time he rounded the corner into the pool complex he'd built up a healthy head of steam. Unfortunately, it didn't stand a chance when faced with the vision of Marcy in one of the smallest bikinis he'd ever seen, stretched out on a lounge chair beside the pool.

He almost swallowed his tongue.

Where the hell had that body come from?

He had seen the woman every single day for the better part of two years. Simon knew that he would have remembered the firm swell of those breasts and the delicate flare of those hips if he'd ever seen them before.

He had the sudden urge to take every single power suit out of her closet and burn them all. They were doing her a grave disservice and he thought it might be his duty to men everywhere to rectify the situation.

Marcy was tiny. But she'd definitely taught him not to judge a book by its cover. That little body packed a punch…he just hadn't realized the punch was aimed straight for his gut.

Simon couldn't help himself; he had to look at her. As his eyes traveled up the length of her body the heavy weight of arousal settled at the base of his spine. With nothing more than a view of her gleaming skin, his cock turned semi-hard. It had been a long time since he'd been embarrassed by an erection—he did not like revisiting the sensation.

But this was Marcy.

And he was supposed to be upset with her.

"You're blocking my light. Could you move?" The soft, lazy tone of her voice was so out of place that it honestly took him several seconds to realize Marcy was the one who'd spoken. Although it wasn't as if there was anyone else around.

Clearing his throat, Simon managed to surreptitiously adjust his fly and desperately tried to dredge up the irritation he'd stomped out here with.

It was damn hard. Along with the rest of him. Especially when she turned to look at him, pulling down her dark tinted sunglasses just far enough to glare at him over the rims. She looked like a pissed-off pixie and he suddenly had the urge to kiss her until she forgot why she was angry.

He bit down onto the inside of his cheek, asking, "What are you doing?" instead.

"I'd think that would be obvious. Sunbathing."

"Sunbathing," he parroted like an idiot. As if the condescending tone of her voice hadn't been bad enough. Shaking his head, and hopefully reawakening his brain, he said, "I mean, why are you out here and not in your office?"

"You fired me, remember?"

"I most certainly did not. I threatened to fire you. Big difference."

"Great, well then, I quit."

"You can't."

"Oh, I can." With a wicked smile on her lips that he'd never seen before, Marcy pushed her glasses back up, pillowed her arms behind her head and leaned back against the lounge chair. The pose stretched her body, pushing the round swell of her breasts against the tiny squares of material covering them. Her stomach muscles pulled tight, drawing his gaze to the tempting little dimple of her belly button.

She was entirely too pleased with herself.

"What's it going to take to get you back to work?"

"Nothing, but an apology never goes out of style. And now that I think about it, I don't believe I've ever heard you say those two little words before."

That was because he really didn't like them.

"I'm sorry," he offered, the words tasting bitter in his mouth. But they were worth it. He'd tell her whatever she wanted to hear, just so long as it meant she'd start handling all the crap in his life so he could focus on his writing.

With a single finger she slid the glasses back down her nose and glared at him again. "That was pathetic, Simon."

He was frustrated, exhausted and slightly sick to his stomach. "What do you want, Marcy?" he bellowed. "I'll give you whatever you want. You have me by the balls—just name your price."

"I don't want your balls, Simon, and I never have."

He reached down and pulled her up out of the chair. He had no idea what he intended to do—maybe march her back inside the building and handcuff her to her desk. Hell, it had worked for his friend and former head of security, Zane. The one and only time Zane had handcuffed someone on the island he'd ended up falling in love with her.

Only, Simon had no intention of falling in love with anyone, least of all Marcy. What he did want was his damn manager back.

"Let go of me," she growled at him, deep in her throat.

"Not on your life."

Somewhere along her upward journey, her glasses had been knocked off. Her eyes blazed. Her face was flushed, not with the warmth of the tropical sun but the passion of her anger.

He found himself letting her go anyway, unwrapping his hands from around her arms slowly. The inside edge of his fingers felt scalded where they'd touched her skin. He wondered if she'd been out in the sun too long, but didn't want to risk touching her again to find out. She didn't look burned....

Once she was free, instead of pulling away as he'd expected, she pushed forward, crowding her body into his space. His chest tightened.

Her pert little nose reached just to the hollow at the base of his throat, but that didn't stop her from spearing him with her gaze. The tips of her breasts, barely covered by the pale yellow excuse for a bathing suit, pressed into the upward curve of his belly. Some sweet, floral scent mixed with sunscreen enveloped her.

The sudden vision of him rubbing the stuff into her soft skin filled his mind. He sucked a breath deep into his lungs, then regretted it when that scent swelled inside him, consuming him from the inside out.

The erection he'd somehow managed to get under control stirred again. Simon took a step backward in order to hide it from her.

"It's about damn time you had to learn how to handle this stuff on your own. I'm tired of watching you gallivant around this place like it's nothing more than a beach oasis that somehow manages to run itself. Maybe if you get a taste of what a single day of my life is like, you'll appreciate whoever comes in to take my place when I am finally gone." She returned to the lounge chair, stretching out.

"I appreciate you."

"Empty words. And since you've given me no choice but to sit here for the next two weeks, I've made it my mission to change that. I consider it my civic duty."

All Simon could think was *Oh, shit.*

MARCY STARED UP AT SIMON. She had to admit the bemused expression on his face was somewhat rewarding.

She wasn't nearly as upset this morning as she'd been yesterday when Simon had announced he had her trapped on the island.

She'd made a phone call to Mr. Bledsoe, the owner of the hotel in New York, and when she'd explained that she was stuck, he'd agreed to arrange a video interview with the selection committee. Tomorrow at 8:30 a.m. with any luck she'd be well on her way to a new position.

In the meantime, she'd decided to take advantage of the resort amenities that she'd never had the opportunity to use before. It had been a long time—a very long time—since she'd sat on her rear and done nothing all day. She had to admit, at first, she'd been a little restless. Sitting idle wasn't in her nature.

She'd gotten the hang of it pretty darn quickly, though. She'd made a huge dent in the Cooper Simmens thriller she'd hoped to read on the plane and had managed to take a little catnap in the sun. As long as she didn't burn, those two activities seemed perfect enough to keep her busy for the next two weeks.

If she could survive Simon.

First, he honestly didn't think he'd done anything wrong by forcing her to stay on the island and screwing up all her plans. He figured he wrote her paycheck, so that made her his slave. Yeah, right.

Second, his frustrating lack of interest in the resort drove her up the wall. He kept saying he had things to do, but in two years she'd never actually *seen* him do anything but mess with his computer, snorkel and surf. It wasn't as if the man had another job. He just wanted this place to make money so he could fool around.

He was constantly locking himself inside the office or taking mysterious trips to the mainland for heaven only knew what—probably to visit his latest lover.

Marcy's right eyelid began to twitch. The thought of him with a lover made her want to snarl, although she realized she had no right to care.

"I do not need a life lesson from you, Marcy. What I need is for you to do your damn job."

"I don't have a job anymore," she responded patiently. How many times would she have to say it before he got it through his thick skull? Just because she was still physically on the island didn't mean he could make her do a darn thing.

He opened his mouth to argue—she could see the stormy cast to his eyes—but a loud explosion rocked the ground beneath their feet, cutting him off before he could say anything else. It was followed by a towering spout of water.

Simon's eyes widened. A series of loud curses and raised voices came from behind the main building.

"What the hell…" he said, moving quickly toward the chaos.

Marcy tried to stay in her chair. She really did. But she just couldn't. Someone might be hurt, and while the appeal of teaching Simon a lesson was great, it couldn't trump her basic human nature.

Grabbing her towel and wrapping it around her body sarong-style, Marcy sprinted after him.

Skidding to a halt, she came inches away from barreling into the solid wall of his back. Considering he was close to a foot taller than she was, he blocked her entire view. However, the pandemonium and the loud hiss of escaping water was enough for her to realize whatever was in front of him wasn't good.

Bracing her hands on Simon's hips for balance, she leaned around him. The scene before her was something out of a comedy—a bad one.

Five big, burly, tattooed men stood around a gushing geyser of water. One of those famous tropical breezes sprayed a fine mist directly into her face.

And beneath her hands she could feel the steady rumble of anger rolling through Simon's body. For the first time she realized that her palms had heated through from the warmth of him. But there was something else, a sizzle of electricity that spiked up her arm and into her body to give her heart a little jolt. Startled by the sensation, Marcy jerked her hands away and scooted out from behind him.

"Don't worry, Mr. Reeves. We'll have this fixed in no time."

"Define no time," he said. From the corner of her eye she could see the glare Simon leveled at the single man who'd been daring enough to step forward from the pack. Although Marcy noticed the other four men had taken a rather large step backward, so it was entirely possible that his newfound status as spokesperson hadn't been intentional.

The worker glanced down at the bubbling water. At least the geyser had eased off. No doubt the pressure of the explosion had bled off the force pushing at the water.

"Um…" He scratched his head and glanced up again without actually looking Simon in the eye. "I think we hit the main waterline, so…" His voice trailed off without him actually committing to a time frame.

"You think? Really? What gave it away? I'm guessing this means you're going to have to shut off the water?"

In some perverse corner in the back of Marcy's mind she had to admit that it was refreshing to see Simon's signature sarcasm leveled at someone else for a change.

The other man nodded slowly. "Yes, sir, so we can work on the line. Anything fed by this line will be without water while we repair it."

An expletive burst from Simon. "That's everything but a few bungalows fed by the old water tanks."

Soon after coming to the island, Simon had upgraded all the outdated plumbing and as much of the electrical as possible. The few bungalows the staff used had been too far back to tie into the new system, so he'd left them on the reservoir.

"How long?"

"One, maybe two days," the other man said, but his tone didn't exactly encourage confidence in the estimate.

"Two days isn't acceptable. We have a business to run."

Marcy decided not to mention that the only person inhabiting that building right now was Simon.

"I expect this fixed no later than five o'clock this afternoon. And if it isn't, you'll work through the night until it is."

"But Mr. Reeves, how do you expect us to work in the dark?"

"I really don't care."

Simon spun on his heel. He stopped midstride, his gaze grabbing Marcy's. His dark blue eyes flashed. For just a second, beneath that laid-back surf-god exterior, Marcy saw the outline of a driven, take-no-prisoners man.

"Don't say a word."

She opened her mouth.

"Not one word."

And closed it again.

Her lips twitched. She tried desperately to keep them straight, but it was a battle she was quickly losing.

With another growl of frustration, he walked away.

Marcy tried to stop the words before they left her lips. Really, she did. But she couldn't seem to help herself.

"See, that wasn't so hard," she called out to his retreating back.

4

SIMON STUMBLED from his desk to the large windows behind him. When had it gotten dark? Stars twinkled overhead, brighter than anything he'd seen when he lived in the city. Palm trees swayed at the edge of the beach and he could almost hear the slush of water as it washed against the sand.

This was a view he'd never get tired of.

A sense of peace stole over him even as he rubbed at his tired eyes. The island had become his sanctuary. Tonight it was quieter than normal. Unlike most only children, he'd never had a problem with sharing what was his, as long as it suited his purposes. And although he'd become pretty adept at tuning out the background noise of the resort guests, it was nice to have the place practically to himself for a change.

Until a loud bang shattered the peace. Five men scrambled around the side of the building, one holding the waistband of his pants tight in a fist so they wouldn't fall as his legs worked overtime. Simon couldn't hear their words, but could definitely see the animated motion of their mouths that suggested they were all yelling.

He closed his eyes. He really didn't want to know.

The sight might have been comical if their scurrying hadn't meant his deadline was no doubt screwed.

He fought back a groan, knowing it wouldn't do any good. Crossing to the small sink at his wet bar, he flipped up the faucet handle and wasn't surprised when a gurgle of air came out.

He needed a shower, some food and a few hours away from his computer so that his brain could recover from the marathon session of writing he'd just finished. Not to mention the words on the screen had started to blur, something that didn't exactly help the creative process.

He had few options. All the guest rooms and cottages operated off the same water system as the main building, so they were out. Along with the apartments above the restaurant, where most of the other staff lived.

The bunkhouse was sourced by the old reservoir system, but he knew if he came in contact with the crew right now they were liable to get an earful…and possibly quit. He didn't need any more of that going around. However, there were several employee bungalows that the highest level of staff used.

Tony and Sara, their dance instructors, used one. The couple had elected to stay on the island during the break and Simon was loath to impose on them, since they were newly married. Xavier had been given Zane's old place, but he was just settling in and, considering the man had already tried to corner him about talking business, Simon had no desire to just drop by and give him an opening for the discussion.

That left Marcy's cottage. Simon stared out the window for several minutes, considering. On one hand, she definitely wouldn't be excited to see him. However, despite the tough outer shell she liked to present to the world, he knew she had a soft-candy center, and he thought she might find it hard to turn him away in his hour of need. Although he'd be the first to admit that he wasn't Marcy's favorite person—at least not at the moment.

Maybe if he buttered her up…

Simon stopped long enough to shut down his computer and lock his office before heading out across the island. He thought about checking on the work crew, but decided ignorant bliss was probably a better option at the moment.

A quick side trip to the wine cellar beneath the restaurant yielded a bottle of wine, a crisp chardonnay he knew was Marcy's favorite. Not that she drank on a regular basis, but the island was small and he tended to pick up on details. He'd seen her leaving the restaurant, the same bottle tucked under her arm, several times over the past two years.

Today that knowledge would come in handy.

The island was dark as he walked along the pebbled path toward the employee cottages at the back of the property. The bar was closed, without the lights, music and laughing guests that usually spilled out of the rustic structure. The soles of his shoes crunched along the path and the tiny hairs at the nape of his neck stood on end.

Oh, what he could do with a scene like this. Someone walking alone at night along the edge of the jungle…

One of the hazards of his job was an overactive

imagination. It was something he'd always had—especially as a child. His mother had explained over and over that there were no monsters under the bed, in the closet, behind the bathroom door or lurking outside his window just waiting for the moment he closed his eyes.

He no longer believed in monsters—at least of the make-believe kind. But he'd done enough research on serial killers, rapists, child molesters and the general dregs of society for him to believe wholeheartedly in the twisted, psychopathic possibilities of the human mind. There were monsters in the world, all right, but they didn't live under the bed. They walked among the rest of humanity, going largely ignored and unnoticed.

Shaking off the eerie sensation, Simon rounded the corner to Marcy's bungalow. Warm lights burned into the night, welcoming. Stepping up onto the small porch that lined the front of her cottage, he couldn't stop himself from peeking inside the large picture window... just to get an idea of what he might be up against.

But what he saw was far from what he expected.

Marcy, in a pair of small gray shorts and a bright blue tank top, was dancing around her small space. The furniture was fairly standard for the island. A large four-poster bed made of rich, warm wood. A small dining table with two chairs set against the far wall of the tiny open kitchen. And a plush sofa in a bright red color that surprised him.

The cord connecting her earbuds to the iPod clipped at her waist jerked in time to her movements as she twisted and turned around the entire place. Simon sucked in a breath when she closed her eyes and nearly slammed into the side of the coffee table. But she somehow managed to miss it.

Her hair was down, her skin flushed from exertion. The tight muscles in her calves and thighs flexed as she bounced around the cottage. Her back arched. The round swell of her breasts swayed beneath the worn cotton of her shirt. She didn't have a bra on.

And suddenly Simon couldn't swallow.

He'd never seen her like this...unfettered, alive, glowing. He should move. Knock on the door. Logically, he realized that. But his feet wouldn't budge. He just stayed there, glued to the worn boards of her front porch, and stared.

Until she spun in front of him. Her eyes popped open and connected with his through the clear glass between them.

He was caught. But right now he didn't care.

Oh, GOD. Marcy was mortified.

Her feet slid against the hardwood floor as she tried to stop her movement midmotion. Her hips were thrust out, her feet pigeon-toed, and her knees collided together in mid gyration.

And Simon just kept staring.

She wasn't a great dancer. In fact, she'd skipped her senior prom because she was afraid of making a fool of herself. You always heard about the awkward girls with long limbs and gangly arms who grew into their bodies and became tall, beautiful supermodels. Well, she hadn't grown into hers. Instead, she'd gotten hit twice—awkward and short.

But she loved music, and whenever she turned it on her body just wanted to move. Her muscles twitched. Her feet flexed. Her shoulders swayed, urging her on. But she always made damn sure that she was alone before she ever gave in.

What the heck was Simon doing here? Interrupting her private time. Spying on her.

Scowling, Marcy shot across the room and snatched open the front door. Apparently he'd recovered enough from the shock of seeing her spastic movements, because he was propped against her doorjamb, a bottle of wine in his outstretched hand.

"I brought you a present."

"What are you doing outside my house in the middle of the night, Simon?"

He frowned, pulling the bottle back against his chest. Pushing away from the frame, his tall, powerful body straightened, towering over her. Marcy felt the urge to take a step back, overwhelmed by more than just the shadow that fell across her. He was too close. And the room was suddenly too warm.

"Come inside," she grumbled, "before you let all the cool air out."

Stepping away, Marcy hoped Simon would close the door behind him…because she really didn't want to reach around him. She didn't like this man, she reminded herself, even as a familiar and unwanted tingle started at the nape of her neck.

Pushing it away, Marcy went on the defensive, stabbing him with the powerful glare she'd learned to use to compensate for her lack of height. People often dismissed her because of her size, but she'd learned to use their underestimation to her advantage.

Unfortunately, that no longer worked with Simon.

"Why were you spying on me?"

"*Spying* is such a harsh word."

"If it looks like a duck and quacks like a duck…"

"I do not waddle," Simon said with mock sarcasm.

Verbal sparring with Simon was like arguing with

a silver-tongued snake. He always managed to talk in circles, never really answering a question unless he wanted to. She'd often wondered if he'd been on the debate team growing up. If he hadn't, it was a shame because he most certainly would have dominated any competition.

Taking a deep breath, Marcy asked, "What do you want?"

The smile he flashed at her was lethal for so many reasons. It was charming, no question. Bright. His eyes lowered just a little whenever he did it, connecting with hers and somehow making the whole thing more personal. As if for that moment she was the most important person in the world.

Unfortunately, she'd seen him use the same tactic many times. He was an equal-opportunity exploiter. The problem was that even though she knew his charm was hollow, it always seemed to knock her sideways a bit. Her heart stuttered. Her brain went a little fuzzy, and she found it difficult to concentrate on whatever they were talking about.

She shook her head, trying to dispel the reaction.

"To borrow your shower. And maybe your kitchen."

"No way." No way in hell. The last thing she needed right now was Simon invading her space. Her sanctuary. The one spot on the entire island she was guaranteed to find some peace because it was solely hers and no one bothered her here.

"Come on. The crew still doesn't have the water back on." He took a step toward her, and then another, crowding into her personal space. Years of refusing to be intimidated by anyone was the only thing that kept her from retreating. "You know you can't refuse someone in distress."

The scent of him overwhelmed her, filling her lungs and invading every molecule of her body as she unintentionally breathed him in. Dark, spicy and all male with a hint of something light and...salty. There was nothing artificial about it—about him. Nothing from a bottle for Simon. Nope, he was all natural.

"I really need a shower." His husky words tripped down Marcy's spine and she found herself swallowing. Hard. Trying to get control of her senses.

He certainly didn't smell in desperate need of a shower, but she wasn't about to point that out right now.

Instead, she licked her lips. She had to. They were bone-dry. And said, "If you're in distress, I'm the tooth fairy."

He didn't hesitate a moment, but popped off a comeback with the straightest face she'd ever seen. "When I'm done with my shower, will you show me your pile of teeth?"

Her lips twitched. Damn it all to hell.

How long could a shower take? Five, ten minutes at the most and then he'd be out of her hair. "Fine," she groaned.

He was halfway across her bungalow before the word had even left her mouth, flashing another one of those damn smiles at her over his retreating back.

"But be quick about it. I have things to do," she added in an assertive growl just to remind them both where they stood.

He disappeared into the bathroom, his voice floating back out at her. "Like more dancing? I wouldn't mind sticking around to watch that show."

"No. No sticking, no show." Her face flushed hot with renewed embarrassment and she was grateful he couldn't see it from the other room.

"That's a shame. I could use some entertainment. It's rather boring in that big building all by myself." He stuck his head back around the frame of the door.

He was naked. At least what she could see of him. All wide shoulders and taut, tanned skin. The swell of well-defined pecs and just the hint of sculpted abs. A sprinkling of golden hair narrowed to a line down the center of his chest to disappear behind the dark wood of the door frame.

Marcy swallowed. Again. It seemed like the only thing she was capable of doing.

"I'm cooking dinner," she blurted to keep from staring, or licking her lips or asking him to walk out of that room so she could see what was hidden behind the door.

What was wrong with her tonight?

Sure, she'd...reacted to Simon before—more than she would have liked, considering he was her boss and she'd been down that road before with disastrous results. But nothing she couldn't handle. Hormones were easily controlled. He was a hot, virile male and it would have been foolish of her to expect *not* to react to him on occasion.

Maybe she was reacting so strongly because he was inside her home. She realized that in all the time she'd worked at Escape, Simon had never once come to her bungalow. That was it. It had to be.

"Dinner? Any hope of sharing? I'm starving and it's a little hard to cook without water."

Jeez, he wanted a lot from her tonight. But he wasn't going to get it.

"Not a snowball's chance in hell."

The loud sound of a zipper going down ripped through her tiny bungalow. Marcy's eyes seemed to bulge for a minute before finding their place back inside her head. He hadn't even bothered to close the door. The man was either mental or incredibly self-confident. Or possibly both.

"Need I remind you that since you quit this morning this bungalow technically no longer belongs to you?"

"Need I remind you that I tried to leave and you wouldn't let me?"

He stuck his head back around the doorway one more time. The problem was now Marcy didn't have to wonder if he was completely naked. She knew. Her mind started doing somersaults and playing tricks. It conjured up images of what he might look like fully exposed.

Unable to take it anymore, Marcy turned her back on the doorway, heading for the kitchen to cover her retreat.

"How about we consider dinner tonight payment for however long you stay?"

"Exactly how long will that be?"

"Until you come to your senses and realize you don't want to quit."

"Not going to happen."

"I brought you wine. The least you can do is feed me."

And, oh, she was going to need that wine because even as her brain said no, her mouth opened and said, "Oh, all right."

The damn man laughed as he ducked back inside the bathroom. This time he closed the door behind him. Thank God.

Although the sound of water rushing through the pipes didn't exactly help her control her wayward thoughts. Instead, it made them worse. The vision of him naked, surrounded by steam, with rivulets of water dripping down his body made her throat feel dry, scratchy and irritated.

Screwing her eyes shut, Marcy concentrated on something else. She pulled some strips of chicken from the freezer, then grabbed bell peppers, onions and squash. Chopping the veggies gave her something else to focus on—and luckily she managed not to nick a finger.

The meat sizzled in the hot skillet. She threw in a splash of soy sauce, Worcestershire and teriyaki marinade along with the veggies. The spicy scent that filled her little kitchen was pleasant and warm and Marcy found a smile curling her lips despite the fact that Simon was only a few feet away.

Cooking was a luxury she didn't often indulge in, but enjoyed. She usually thought it silly to spend the time herself when a five-star restaurant was only a few steps away from her front door. The chef was excellent, and who wouldn't appreciate gourmet meals every night?

But there was something reassuring and relaxing about making her own meal, simple as it was.

While everything cooked, she popped the cork on the bottle Simon had brought and poured a glass of wine. As an afterthought, she pulled down another glass and poured him one, as well. Maybe it would mellow them both out enough that they'd end the night without wanting to kill each other.

She threw together a simple salad of greens, tomatoes and cucumbers.

And then waited.

And waited.

And wondered what the heck was taking him so

long. His hair might be longer than some guys, but it wasn't as if it was down to his waist and needed extra conditioning. So it was a little shaggy against his collar....

He didn't have a razor or toothbrush. Hell, she realized, he hadn't even brought a change of clothes.

She stirred the chicken for lack of anything better to do. And found herself staring at the closed door... imagining.

5

Simon would never take warm water for granted again. The muscles running from the back of his neck down to the base of his spine ached from too much hunching over the keyboard. He hadn't realized how tense he'd become until the pounding warmth had released the knots.

He probably spent a good five minutes just standing idle beneath the spray, his mind going in pleasant, unproductive circles that he couldn't ignore.

Reaching down for the shampoo bottle sitting on a small ledge, he squirted a purple glob of the stuff into the palm of his hand. Without thought, he dumped it over the crown of his head and started rubbing.

Only to be knocked sideways when Marcy's scent overwhelmed him. It was lavender and vanilla, somehow feminine, sweet and powerful all at the same time. Not because of the actual scents but because for the past two years they'd always reminded him of her.

His body responded, his cock leaping to attention with a speed that shocked him. Need, deep and pulsing, whipped through his body and he closed his eyes tight trying to ignore it.

This had been a bad idea.

But there was nothing he could do about it now. He was here, held hostage in Marcy's bathroom by a raging erection and a desire to possess her that had blindsided him. Well, okay, maybe not blindsided, but surprised him at the very least.

Gritting his teeth, Simon looked around for a bar of soap and realized there wasn't one. Squinting at the row of bottles, he picked out one that promised silky-smooth skin and popped the lid, bringing it experimentally to his nose. Lavender. Again.

He hadn't thought to grab a washcloth. What kind of person didn't have a bar of soap in the shower? The only thing that remotely resembled something useful was a big puffy thing hanging from a hook over the showerhead. He'd seen them before, in other women's bathrooms, but never stopped long enough to care what they were for. Nine times out of ten, he'd been otherwise occupied and neither party involved had been worried about getting clean. They'd been concentrating on being very, very dirty.

Simon slammed his jaws together as a vision of Marcy, her tight little body wrapped around his waist and her back pressed against the wall of the shower, burst through his mind.

Okay, no puffy thing. Instead, he squeezed the soap out into his hand and began lathering it across his skin. He was going to smell like a pansy when this was over. But maybe that would keep him from acting on the throbbing hard-on jutting out from his hips.

He studiously ignored that entire area on the idea that pretending it wasn't there was the best course of

action. Although that seemed pointless since the lather
slipped down his body anyway to part around his erection and slide over his tight balls.

With a hiss through his teeth, Simon gave up. Rins-
ing the soap from his body, he slammed the faucet off
and jumped from the confining walls of the shower.
Unfortunately, even the towel he grabbed from beneath
the sink smelled like lavender.

Did the woman own stock in the stuff?

Simon reached for the clothes he'd thrown haphazardly into a pile on the stool sitting in the corner of the
room. The fly on his shorts pressed painfully against
the ridge of his uncooperative cock. He reached down
and tried to adjust for a more comfortable fit, but there
wasn't one. The ache was endless.

With a snarl, he pulled his shirt back over his shoulders, leaving the tail untucked and dangling to hide the
bulge. And started thinking unpleasant thoughts.

Starving children in Africa.

Stinging bees.

The workmen outside who hadn't managed to fix
the water.

He waited for the erection to go away.

And waited some more.

Finally he realized it wasn't going anywhere and
that if he didn't get out of this bathroom Marcy was
going to think he'd drowned. And come in after him.
His eyes strayed over to the shower and the drops of
water that peeled slowly down the pane of glass. Despite all his efforts, the vision of her in there with him
returned with a vengeance.

Which would not be good.

Snatching the knob, Simon ripped open the door
and walked back out into Marcy's living area. He was

greeted by a tantalizing smell. Thank god it wasn't lavender.

"Jeez, how much primping can one man do?"

Simon stared at her for several seconds, his brain spinning uselessly on her words. Until he realized what she was talking about. Perhaps her low opinion of him—and apparently his vanity—could work in his favor here.

"It takes a lot of effort to maintain this level of perfection."

"Please." Marcy's lips twitched down on one corner. "Half the time you look like you dragged the first thing out of the closet that you came to. You've needed a haircut for months. Pretty soon no one will be able to see those beautiful blue eyes behind the shaggy blond hair."

"You think my eyes are beautiful," he teased, flashing her a wide grin.

She groaned and looked at the ceiling as if hoping for help. Her eyes sparkled, just like the water outside their little island when the sun hit it just right. Her jaw tightened, flexing in a way that made him ache to give her another workout for that mouth.

"Your ego is a constant amazement to me, do you know that?"

"My ego? That isn't usually what women compliment me on."

"That wasn't a compliment."

"Sure sounded like one to me. Didn't you just say I amazed you?"

With a huff, Marcy turned and grabbed a glass of wine from the counter. The contents sloshed over the side. She reached out, snatched one of his hands, pulled it close to her body and slapped the glass against his palm.

"Drink," she ordered. "At least that'll keep your mouth occupied for a while."

His eyes unerringly strayed to her mouth. Those full lips, more often than not pulled into a tight line of frustration or concentration, were now parted. He could see the delicate pink inside her mouth and wanted to dive in and taste it for himself. He leaned closer, although he couldn't remember consciously deciding to do it.

Marcy's eyes widened. The pulse at the base of her throat began to throb and he could feel the answering echo as it shot straight to his groin. That tantalizing tongue darted out to scrape across her open lips. Simon's eyes narrowed, focusing totally on the prize that he wanted—her mouth.

With an almost inaudible gasp, Marcy turned away, breaking the connection that had caught them both.

Simon studied her as she quickly dished food from the pan on the stove onto two beautiful plates. They were thick, heavy and, on closer inspection, Simon realized probably handmade. Indigo and burgundy swirled across the surface in an abstract pattern. They were definitely not island issue, but something she'd brought with her to Île du Coeur.

And he realized it was the first touch of something personal he'd seen. Her office had no photographs, no knickknacks, no little baskets or cartoony staplers. Everything was silver, stark and professional.

Her hands were steady now, but he was almost certain they hadn't been when she'd first turned around. He'd been seducing women since puberty, so he knew the signs of interest well enough. Hell, he had the perfect tutorial outside his front door. Every night at the resort some man—or woman—was making the moves hoping to end up in someone else's bed.

Although he really didn't need the lessons.

Marcy wanted him. Physically at least. Of that he was damn sure. She might not like it, but that didn't change the facts.

She brushed past him and a blast of lavender hit him square in the face.

His body responded.

Marcy studiously ignored him as she ate her dinner. Simon, on the other hand, studiously watched her. And the more he watched the more agitated she became.

A tiny smile tugged at the edge of his lips as he slipped a piece of chicken into his mouth. She really was a good cook. He had no idea why that surprised him, but it did.

"This is excellent," He said finally, breaking the tense silence that had settled between them.

"It's nothing."

"No, it's simple and good. I didn't realize you could cook."

"There's a lot about me you don't know, Simon," she said, looking up into his eyes for the first time since she'd sat down across from him.

He quirked a single eyebrow. "Like what? Enlighten me."

"Maybe I don't want to."

Simon set his fork on his plate and leaned across the table. He stared into her azure eyes—they were so bright and clear. Such an unusual shade that he was sure she'd learned long ago to use to her advantage. She wanted to look away. He could see it in the way the corners of her eyes compressed. But she wouldn't.

Instead, she lowered her chin and silently challenged him in that frustrating way of hers.

But he was no coward and actually enjoyed the provocation. "Why not? What are you afraid of? It isn't like I'm asking you to strip naked in front of me. Just tell me where you learned to cook."

Her skin flushed a soft pink the minute the word *strip* left his mouth. But her eyes flashed and her lips thinned and he knew she'd rise to the bait.

"I taught myself. I lived most of my life in premier hotels with just my father. And while he was a wonderful man and a great father, he was a terrible cook. He'd always say that not taking advantage of the gourmet meals available to us was tantamount to committing a sin."

"Not very religious, your father, then, hmm?" he asked.

Marcy reached up and ran her hands through her hair, ruffling her bangs. The soft blond strands settled back around her face in a disheveled mess that did nothing to dampen the buzz of attraction fighting through his blood. His fingers curled against his palm, the only way to keep him from reaching out to brush the wisps away from her cheeks.

She was uncomfortable. Simon wondered if it was sharing part of her background and life that made her so, or if it was specifically sharing those details with him that flustered her.

"So why did you learn to cook? I thought you'd spent most of your adult life living in a hotel, as well."

"I did." Marcy's lips twisted into a self-deprecating semblance of a smile. "This place—" she looked around, but her gaze returned to him and Simon felt a tiny thrill blossom in the center of his chest when she did "—was the first time I'd ever had access to a kitchen, actually."

"Wait," he said. "Are you saying you taught yourself to cook while you've been living here?"

When had she done that? And for heaven's sake, why? "What's wrong with our restaurant? And why haven't you fixed it?"

"Nothing," she asserted. "There's nothing wrong with the restaurant. We get rave reviews and our chef has an excellent reputation."

Simon's eyebrows beetled. He didn't understand. "Then what in the world made you take up cooking?"

She looked away again. "I don't know. I was bored, I guess. There really isn't a lot to do after I leave the office. I'm not much for TV or movies. I guess I was used to a big city with lots of museums and theaters and social events." Her eyes wandered back and she shrugged. "It filled the time. And I discovered I was good at it. Sort of surprised me."

A smile, gentle and unlike anything he'd ever seen on her face before, curved her lips. "Dad always said my mom was an excellent cook."

There was a vulnerability there that made the center of his stomach twist uncomfortably. While he liked this softer side to Marcy, he wasn't used to it and didn't know what to do with it. *Vulnerable* was the last word he'd ever use to describe the tiny bulldog that normally ran his resort. *Capable, fearless, dominating, frustrating, enticing*…these were all words he would have used.

Searching for familiar ground, Simon grabbed on to something she'd said. "What do you mean there isn't any entertainment on the island? We have plenty!"

"Sure, if I was interested in a weekend fling with some stranger. And that's assuming said stranger wasn't just looking for T and A." Marcy looked down at her own body and frowned. "It isn't like I fit the stereotypical mold for that sort of thing."

"Putting aside your derogatory view of our guests, any man who doesn't jump at the chance to sleep with you is an idiot. You're beautiful."

Marcy blinked, appearing nonplussed. It was a new look for her, one he liked for some reason. Maybe it made her more human than he was used to her being. She was Marcy. Efficient, unflappable Marcy. But he'd made her stumble.

"I...you..." She sputtered before finding her footing. "Thank you. I think."

They stared at each other for several seconds. Simon realized that at some point in their conversation they'd moved closer to each other, both leaning over the table that separated them. Whether from the heat of their argument or the awareness pulsing relentlessly beneath his skin, it really didn't matter. The result was the same.

He wanted her.

And for the first time since she'd stepped foot on his island, he couldn't remember why that was a bad idea.

Oh yeah, she worked for him.

Or, rather, she had.

Past tense. Not anymore. Which meant there was no reason to deny what he wanted.

The fantasy that had been haunting him since he'd opened that damn bottle of shampoo burst through his brain again.

He wanted Marcy. And he was a man who usually got what he wanted.

MARCY HAD NO IDEA what was going on behind those devilish blue eyes, but whatever it was made her…uncomfortable. In fact, she'd been uncomfortable since the moment Simon walked through her door.

She reached up and fiddled with the straps of her tank top. Why was she suddenly so hot? The stove. That's what it was.

In a flurry of activity, Marcy began clearing the dishes off the table. The mundane chore allowed her to not only turn her back on Simon and the effervescent feeling he stirred in the pit of her stomach, but also to hopefully speed up his departure.

Dinner was over. He'd had a shower. And now he could leave.

Marcy's lips were suddenly dry and tight. She ran her tongue across them to try to find some relief. It didn't help.

Frowning, she turned back to grab another handful of dishes and nearly collided with Simon. His hands were full of her favorite dishes, so he couldn't reach out and steady her. Instead, he jerked the plates above their heads and pressed the line of his body against hers, giving her a solid surface to rest against.

That rolling, bubbling sensation in her stomach erupted, spilling through her entire body. Her skin tingled from the inside out, the tiny hairs running down her arms standing at attention.

She'd never in her life responded that way to a man touching her. It was overwhelming and she didn't like it at all.

Taking a step back, she put much-needed space between them. Simon simply followed, towering above her. She was sensitive to her small stature, sometimes overly sensitive. But she was used to people—especially men—looming over her. She didn't let it bother her. She couldn't afford that kind of weakness, not in the hotel business, where she had to handle not only prickly executives but also pushy guests.

Simon bothered her. Standing in front of her, his body curved slightly as if he could completely engulf her at any moment… She wanted to fidget, to slip out from under him and stand on her tiptoes. But that would show her vulnerability and she refused to do that.

Instead, she dropped her head back and stared up, up, up into his eyes. She would not let him intimidate her.

He set the plates onto the counter on either side of her. His arms stretched around her as he leaned closer. Her lungs filled with that damn scent—crisp and clean and somehow wild…. Although tonight there was something new beneath it, floral and sweet. The combination made her picture the two of them together. Naked. She tried to hold her breath so she wouldn't pull any more in. Surely now that his hands were empty, he'd move away.

But he didn't.

Instead, he gripped the counter. The heat of his body melted into her. It should have been irritating, but instead, her muscles responded. They went lax and she was suddenly glad for the edge of the counter that pressed into the small of her back and kept her from hitting the floor.

Marcy swallowed and looked up into Simon's eyes again. Her throat went dry at what she saw there. They were dark, the smoldering blue almost completely obscured by his expanding pupils. Gone was the jovial, irreverent expression that seemed to be his constant companion, replaced by a calculating intensity that scared her senseless.

She wanted to say something. To make him stop looking at her that way because it made her body do unfamiliar and uncontrollable things. A throbbing ache settled at the apex of her thighs.

This was not good.

She wanted to move, but she couldn't. Her feet were frozen to the floor.

His eyes searched her face, for what she wasn't sure, but whatever it was he found it. Leaning closer, he nuzzled the curve where her neck and shoulder met. No, *nuzzle* was the wrong word. He didn't actually touch her, but she could feel him there.

The drag of air across her skin as he pulled it deep into his lungs was almost more devastating than if he'd actually touched her. That she could have fought against. At least, that's what she told herself.

"Lavender," he whispered, the word stirring strands of her hair as they tickled her cheek.

Her lips fell open. She couldn't help herself. Her mouth tingled and pulsed with a need she didn't want.

His lips pressed against hers. He didn't overwhelm her as she might have expected he would. He didn't even press inside the open invitation of her mouth. Instead, he simply savored the connection, brushing his mouth lightly across hers.

Her fingers tightened around the counter. She wanted to reach for him, but still had enough brainpower to realize that was a bad idea. One step a little too far.

As kisses went…it was disappointing. Not because it wasn't devastating, but because it was. It was so perfect and sweet, so unexpected, that Marcy found herself wishing it would go on forever. And it didn't. That was the disappointing part.

He sighed as he pulled away from her. His eyes were heavy lidded, sexy. They glittered at her with a heat that belied the softness of what he'd just done.

Simon wanted her.

It was obvious.

And her body agreed. It wanted to do whatever he wanted. Lightning sensations licked across her skin, crackling and zinging and making it hard to catch her breath.

"Thank you for dinner," he said, taking a small step away.

This time when her hands clenched it was because she wanted to reach out and pull him back to her. To plaster him full-length along her naked skin and rub against him in an effort to find some relief for the fire he'd built deep in her belly.

But she didn't. Instead, she nodded her head and watched as he walked away.

The quiet click of the door was like a gunshot, finally galvanizing her into action. She crossed her home in three strides, snatched the door open and rushed out onto the tiny covered porch.

He was already several feet down the path leading back to the main buildings of the resort. But he must have heard the sound of her door, because he stopped and turned to look at her.

The island was dark, the moon only a sliver that did little to dispel the night. His entire face was in shadow, but somehow his eyes still managed to flash.

His body, usually loose and languid, was straight and tight. She could see the tension in his muscles as he

took one step toward her. She knew what he thought—
that she'd rushed outside to stop him from leaving.

Instead, she shook her head, one quick motion that
had him pulling up short.

There were a lot of questions swimming around
inside her head. She didn't know which ones to ask.
Which ones she really wanted an answer to. She settled
for the most obvious—and hopefully the least dangerous.

"Why did you do that?" Her voice was low and
rough, almost unrecognizable to her own ears.

His white teeth flashed in the darkness, their quick
appearance her only indication of his smile. It was the
first thing that felt familiar. She'd seen it often, that
irreverent, self-deprecating, unapologetic twist of his
lips that usually drove her crazy because she knew it
wasn't real.

Taking several steps backward, he finally answered,
"Because I wanted to."

6

"BECAUSE I WANTED TO," Marcy grumbled to herself. Of course he did. The man didn't care what anyone else wanted or thought. Did he ask her first if he could kiss her? No. He just went ahead and took what he wanted.

Marcy, after a restless night of tossing and turning, was building up a healthy head of steam. She was also trying to convince herself that if he had asked first she would have said no.

But the little voice inside her head called her a liar. She ignored it.

The problem was that he didn't really want her. He didn't find her sexy. If he had, he would have shown some sign of it before now.

She ignored the *hypocrite* that reverberated through her brain. She'd been fighting her own awareness of the man for the past two years and hadn't given any indication of it. At least until last night.

He just wanted to fluster her. To set her off center. He probably hoped to use her reaction in some hare-brained attempt to convince her to come back to work.

It wasn't going to happen.

Her interview had gone very well this morning. It had been difficult considering her laptop screen was small and four people—Mr Bledsoe, and three of his executives—had been present. But they'd asked tough questions and she was happy with her answers.

And to make sure Simon couldn't convince her to do something stupid—like stay—she intended to get as far away from the resort as physically possible.

Grabbing a tattered backpack from her closet, Marcy filled it with several things—a soft blanket, some paperbacks, a couple sandwiches, snacks and several bottles of water. Beneath the cutoff jean shorts and stretch-necked T-shirt, she wore her bathing suit. Including yesterday, she could count on one hand the number of times she'd worn the thing since coming to the island.

Over the next few days she planned to remedy that.

Starting with a hike out to the waterfall tucked into the heart of the jungle on the uninhabited side of the island. How many times had she heard the guests gushing about the beauty of the secluded spot? How many times had she pointed a couple to the head of the path and promised them a wonderful time?

The problem was she had to take everyone else's assurances of that because she'd never made the time to go there herself. As if she ever had an afternoon free for hiking. Or a massage or a ballroom lesson or a few quiet hours on the beach.

She flung the pack over one shoulder. Habit had her reaching for the two-way radio that sat on the charger on the small table next to the door. Her fingers brushed across the plastic before she caught herself. Pulling her hand back and cradling it against her body as if it had been burned, she stared at the thing.

Taking it would be smart. It was unusual for anyone to get lost out in the jungle, but it did happen. Just a few months ago, Colt and Lena, guests who were being photographed for an Escape ad campaign, had been stuck out there overnight. And she was hiking alone. Being able to contact Xavier if there was an emergency wouldn't be a bad idea.

And if anything else came across the radio, she'd simply turn the volume down. She didn't have to respond or pay attention.

Reaching out with a lightning motion, Marcy palmed the thing and stuffed it into the front pocket before she could change her mind.

A few minutes later the soft trill of birds and the muted chatter of unseen animals welcomed her. It was decidedly cooler beneath the cover of the trees—not that the days were sweltering or anything. While fall didn't bring the change of seasons she'd grown used to in New York, there was a difference, however small.

The biggest problem they had at this time of year was hurricanes, which was one of the reasons they always closed the resort during the fall. While they offered lots of discounts to appeal to frugal travelers, quite a few of them resisted the Caribbean and the potential for their dream vacation to turn into a nightmare with torrential rains and damaging winds. So it wasn't difficult for the resort to carve out two weeks for routine maintenance and repairs, as well as staff vacations.

They'd been lucky lately and hadn't dealt with any major storms in several years. But she knew the island had taken some pretty major hits in the past. The resort had even been closed at one time because of damage the previous owner couldn't afford to fix.

But Marcy wasn't worried about storms, not surrounded by the thickness of the jungle. The tension that had stretched across her shoulders began to ease. She took a deep breath and held it in her lungs. Everything smelled moist, green and vibrant.

The sudden urge to hurry overtook her and she began to run. The balls of her feet barely touched the ground before springing up again. The exercise felt great, something she'd definitely been neglecting in her work-focused fog. Her muscles protested after a little while—there was no question she was slightly out of shape.

She was going to fix that, though, as soon as she got back to New York. She was going to make a few changes in her priorities, starting with taking better care of herself. Although she had to admit staring at the nondescript walls of a gym would have little appeal after the natural beauty of the jungle.

Marcy heard the waterfall long before she saw it. The path became lighter and lighter, making her realize just how dark and dense the jungle had been around her. Breaking through the opening at the end of the path, she stopped to take it all in.

Despite the force of the water breaking against the rocks below, the entire place had a sense of…quiet. It was old, powerful. Marcy let her eyes wander for a few moments, taking everything in. The water looked inviting, but she wasn't ready for a swim.

Her eyes were drawn to the top of the falls. That's where she wanted to go. From up there she'd be able to see everything.

It took her almost twenty minutes to walk around the collecting pool to the far side of the falls and the only way up she could find. The rocks were a little slippery from the wayward spray of the water, but she managed to climb up safely.

There was a small patch of grass, more lush than anything below, spongy and soft. She slipped off her shoes and socks and wiggled her toes. The thick blades tickled the bottom of her feet. Sunlight, unfettered by the trees surrounding the area, fell directly over the patch.

Dropping her pack, Marcy took out the blanket and spread it in the sunshine. Her original plan was to read her book, but she barely got a few pages in before exhaustion stole through her body, weighting her limbs and eyelids.

She closed her eyes and tipped her head back. The underside of the leaves above her looked down. The loud roar of the water faded to background noise. A smile touched the corners of her lips and just as she drifted off to sleep an image of Simon popped into her head.

Towering over her—when didn't he?—he watched her with that same intense, smoldering gaze he'd used on her last night. And this time when he kissed her, he didn't pull away. And she didn't tell him to stop.

Instead, he slowly, deliberately drove her mad.

So much for escaping him in the jungle.

SIMON CROUCHED next to Marcy, running a single finger down the scrunched bridge of her nose. Even in sleep she looked frustrated. Wasn't a nap in the sunshine supposed to ease that kind of stress?

Her skin was soft. It smoothed out beneath his fingers, her entire face easing. The corners of her lips twitched and she rolled her head closer against his hand. His palm cupped her cheek, the warmth of her sun-warmed skin seeping into him. She mumbled something that he couldn't catch and then sighed his name.

Need, hard and sharp, twisted deep inside. He wanted to startle her awake, to strip her bare and take her here on the soft patch of grass. Resisting, he dropped to his knees beside her and went slowly, letting his fingers tickle across the exposed curve of her shoulder. The neck of her T-shirt was stretched out, pulled tight on one side and hanging halfway down her shoulder on the other.

Tiny freckles dotted her skin. They were cute and unexpected. He wanted to reach down and kiss every single one, but refrained. He trailed his fingers up her throat. Even in sleep, she moved toward him, revealing more skin for him to play with.

Her eyes fluttered beneath closed lids and her soft pink lips parted. Reaching with the other hand, he let it trail softly down the outside curve of her thigh. Circling her knee, he moved back up. Her legs were toned and tanned, although he had no idea when she took the time to sit in the sun. At least, not before the past two days.

She rolled beneath his caress, parting her legs and opening herself to him as he moved higher. A brief spurt of guilt shot through him, but he pushed it away. He had no intention of taking advantage of her. Although her unconscious response to him was gratifying. And probably more real than anything she'd shown him before now.

At least now he knew for sure that he hadn't been mistaken last night, or so overrun by his own lust that he'd imagined something that wasn't really there.

His fingers bumped along a small, jagged scar that

ran diagonally up the inside of her thigh. Feeling by touch, he realized it was almost two inches long. He wondered what had happened.

Without thought, he leaned over and placed his lips to the spot. It was a bad idea. She gasped, her body quivering beneath his mouth. Her skin was warm against his lips, soft and inviting. The strings from the hem of her cutoffs tickled his face, reminding him just how close his mouth was to what was hidden beneath.

Her feet scissored and tension tightened her muscles. It was his first clue that she was awake.

Turning his head, he kept his mouth close to the temptation of her body and looked up into her face. She stared down at him, her eyes now bright and vivid, definitely awake.

"What are you doing?" she whispered, her voice thick with sleep.

"Kissing it and making it better?" he asked, arching one eyebrow.

She moved again beneath him, not in an attempt to push him away, but in a restless motion that he understood. The same need crawled through his body, making his skin feel tight.

"That healed a long time ago."

"What happened?" The heat of her body seeped into his open lips, making them ache to touch her again.

"I dropped a knife. It cut me on the way down."

Had she done that here? A vision of her first clumsy attempts at cooking made his chest tighten. "When?"

"I was twelve."

He hated the idea of her in pain. His fingers brushed softly over the puckered skin. But at least she hadn't injured herself on his watch without him even knowing about it.

Rising on her elbows, Marcy twisted and pulled herself out from under him. He let her go, knowing it wouldn't be for long. Not if he had his way and he could convince her to give in to what her body obviously wanted. From where he'd been, he could smell the heady scent of her arousal.

"What are you doing here, Simon?"

"Looking for you."

"Why?"

He decided not to answer her question. He didn't want to. He wasn't entirely sure what the answer was anyway. From the window in his office he'd watched her walk into the jungle this morning. He knew where she was going. And for the rest of the morning, while he should have been concentrating, he'd been thinking about her.

Fantasies shared space with concern, knowing she was out in the jungle alone. There were snakes and jaguars and high cliffs. And while Marcy was one of the most capable people he'd ever met, she wasn't invincible.

Finally, after finishing a chapter, printing it out and adding it to the pile of work he'd already done, he gave in to the urge to follow her. The day was nice and warm. He wasn't accomplishing much anyway. Maybe if he burned up some of this need and energy he'd be able to concentrate again.

But he wasn't about to tell her that.

"You said my name."

"What?" she asked, confusion clouding her eyes.

"In your sleep. You said my name."

Her eyes widened with shock for just a moment before she hid her reaction. "I did not."

"You did. I promise."

She scoffed. "Please, a promise from you isn't worth the breath it's uttered with."

"That hurts."

She shrugged. "The truth usually does."

"I think I liked you better when you were asleep."

He expected her to make some snappy comeback. It was what they did—verbally spar. He was beginning to think all that aggression had just been an outlet for the sexual frustration that ran between them like a live wire.

Instead, she looked at him and said, "Liar. Right now you're trying to figure out the fastest way into my pants."

He rocked back on his heels. She'd surprised him. The wheels in his brain spun as he tried to figure out the best response to her candor. He wasn't sure there was one, so he decided to match her honesty.

"You wanna save me the trouble and just tell me?"

She laughed. Sunshine washed across her face and her eyes sparkled. He wasn't sure if it was from the direct light or from something more…something internal. He hoped it was more.

Her laughter eased, but even as her gaze connected with his again her body continued to quiver with fettered mirth. "No, I don't think I do."

Pushing herself up from the ground, she grasped the blanket that he still knelt on and yanked against it. It barely budged, but that didn't stop her from trying again.

Simon rose and watched as she folded it, making sure each corner matched and the final product was perfectly square. Stuffing the blanket in, she zipped her pack and moved to fling it over her shoulder. Reaching out, he snagged it from the air. Her body jerked against the unexpected weight as the pack fell suspended between them.

Using it to reel her closer, Simon stepped into her space. His eyes snagged on her mouth and he did nothing to hide his fascination. He watched as her lips jerked, almost parting, before she clamped them into a tight line.

Slowly he let his gaze travel up to her eyes. He stared at her, watching as emotions flitted through the bright blue centers. She was fighting a war that she couldn't win. But he knew she was damn well going to try.

And that was going to be part of the fun.

While he'd never been one to look a gift horse—or willing woman—in the mouth, there was something about Marcy that stirred more than just his libido. This push-and-pull thing that they had going excited him in a way nothing else had in a very long time.

Not even his work. And that cost him a lot to admit.

"You want me, Marcy. Why don't you save us both a lot of misery and just admit it?"

He didn't touch her. He didn't try to influence her. He wanted this to be her decision, her capitulation.

Licking her lips, she said, "What woman wouldn't? You're sexy as hell and you know it. You use your charm and those laid-back bedroom eyes like weapons. But you've never used them on me. Why now?"

She would ask that. She would want to understand all the angles, to analyze and inspect and pick apart the options and reasons before making a decision.

"We're here. You don't work for me anymore…."

Her decision flashed through her eyes long before it left her lips, but that was all the encouragement Simon needed. He reached for her, jerking her full-length against his body.

In his arms she felt small and delicate. There was a disconnect between his perception of her and the reality. She wasn't fragile, but it was easy to forget just how tiny she really was.

He dived in and devoured her. Their mouths met and melted together. He'd expected their first real kiss would have an edge of aggression, as their words usually did. He was wrong.

There was heat and urgency. Need. His tongue scraped against hers, shooting sparks through his entire body. Her gasp of surprise blasted against his open mouth. She tasted like oranges, chocolate and lavender all mixed together.

His hand fisted at the nape of her neck, dragging her head back so he could get more. With the other, he grasped her waist and pulled her up his body. She wrapped her legs firmly around his waist, anchoring them together and, more important, telling him she wanted this just as much as he did.

Her palms pressed against his chest, curling in and urging him closer. She ripped her head out of his hold, squeezing her thighs to push herself higher up his body. She was looming over him, and for the first time since he'd met her, he had to tip his head back to keep up with her.

She pushed in and took what she wanted. Her fingers grasped the side of his head and held him as she matched him thrust for thrust, the heat of her mouth over his as devastating as anything he'd ever experienced before.

He should have expected her to be as much of an

aggressor with sex as she was with everything else. Although it actually surprised him. He was used to women taking a backseat and letting him lead. It was sort of exhilarating and liberating to have her fight him for control.

But he wasn't about to give in. Taking several steps, he set her back against the closest tree. Shade, a cool breeze and anticipation had a shudder quaking through him.

She made a tiny sound in the back of her throat that he swallowed, the first piece of her he planned to claim. With the weight of her body resting against the trunk, his hands were free to explore. Pushing against the hem of her shirt, they scraped up the soft skin of her belly.

Her muscles jumped beneath his touch.

She writhed against him, the apex of her open thighs pressing tight to his aching erection. Denim had never seemed so thick and annoying in his life. He leaned into her, pinning her hips hard against the tree, looking for relief.

"Simon."

The radio he'd been forced to bring with him, since he was apparently in charge, squawked at his hip. He ignored it. Or tried to.

Dragging his hands higher, he wanted to cup her breasts, to fill his palms with her soft round curves. He never made it. She stopped him, slamming her own hands over his with the thin layer of her shirt between them.

Pulling back, she looked at him. "Are you going to get that?" Her words were breathy. Her lungs worked hard beneath his palms, her ribs expanding and contracting in a tantalizing way that made his hand slip against her skin.

"No." Was she crazy? Whatever catastrophe Xavier wanted to tell him about could wait. For an hour. Or maybe until tomorrow if he had his way.

"Simon!"

The screech was louder, and somewhere behind them it echoed.

With her legs still wrapped tight around his waist, the tempting center of her sex pressed against his throbbing cock, she raised a single eyebrow. Her blond hair, in complete disarray thanks to his desperate fingers, clouded around her disapproving face.

With a sigh he extricated a hand—but only one—and reached for the radio at his hip. Pressing the button, he growled, "This better be important."

Marcy's eyes flashed. He rocked his hips against her and relished her soft gasp and the way the azure depths clouded with passion once again.

But they didn't stay that way. Not when Xavier's voice floated between them.

"We've got a problem."

"I hope so, or you're about to get fired."

Marcy's lips twisted.

"Apparently the construction crew managed to get water on the main electrical panel."

"Holy crap," he muttered. "Are they completely incompetent?"

He realized it was the wrong thing to say, because Marcy began to squirm against him—and not in a good way. She was no longer overcome by passion. She wanted down. Now.

She pushed against his shoulders and dropped her legs from around his waist. Her body hung suspended between him and the tree, her toes dangling at least half a foot off the ground.

Damn it. With a frown of his own, he wrapped an arm around her waist and lowered her gently to the ground. So much for picking up where they'd left off. Although he wasn't about to just let her walk away.

Keeping her tight against his body, he asked, "What's the damage?"

"One of the crew was shocked, but he seems to be okay. Dazed."

That didn't seem so bad. Not that he wanted anyone injured, but if the man was conscious, it couldn't be life-threatening. Unfortunately, their on-staff doctor had left with most of the employees.

Xavier's voice crackled again through the connection. "And somehow a small electrical fire started. I've implemented fire protocol, but most of the staff is gone."

Before Xavier could even finish, Marcy was jerking out of Simon's hold. Grabbing her abandoned pack, she flung it over her shoulder and started down the path at a fast clip. Simon was right on her heels.

From out of nowhere another radio appeared in her hand. It was a nice trick, although Simon assumed it had been in her pack and was probably the source of the echo he'd heard. Not the cavern of the falls as he'd assumed.

"Xavier, how big is the fire? What buildings are in danger? Is someone getting the pumper truck?"

"Not big. Luckily, the panel is at the back of the main building and so far the only thing on fire is a small shed. I've called for the truck…but it won't do us much good. The water's out, remember."

Simon let out a long line of expletives. Could this get any worse?

"Oh, and the power's out all over the resort."

Why had he asked?

7

SHE'D NEVER SEEN SIMON move so quickly. His long legs ate up ground and he quickly passed her on the trail back to the resort. A hike that had taken her almost thirty minutes took ten at the fastest sprint she'd ever done. And still she arrived in the middle of the chaos minutes after Simon had.

Along the way, she'd heard him instruct Xavier to hook up the truck to the reservoir system that was still functioning. Unfortunately, that meant the truck was limited in how far the hose could reach. And by the time they'd gotten everything hooked up, the shed was completely engulfed.

It held discarded furniture, decorations and pieces that weren't used but were still in decent shape and worth keeping. No one would be devastated by the loss. The biggest concern was the proximity of the flames to the main hotel building. If that caught fire…it would be bad. Their normal emergency response team was severely limited.

The few employees left on the island crowded around, trying to pitch in and help as best they could.

Xavier stood at the end of the powerful hose, his legs spread wide and his weight grounded as he fought to keep the water trained where they needed it most.

Soot and sparks shot into the air, forming a dangerous dark cloud above them. Red-orange flames licked relentlessly up all four sides of the shed, devouring the worn wood with a crackle and hiss.

And Simon was in the thick of it.

Marcy watched as he issued instructions to the people standing around. With a few terse words he had order evolving out of the chaos. Another team hooked up a second hose to the truck and began spraying the side of the main building.

Two more men jumped in line behind Xavier, making it easier to control the powerful stream of water blasting the building.

Her heart thumped erratically against her chest when Simon rushed toward the fire. "What are you doing?" she shouted just as he slipped around the far side of the shed, way too close to the fingers of the fire for her comfort.

Idiot! She wanted to scream at the top of her lungs, but she didn't. He wouldn't hear her anyway above the noise of the truck and the sizzle of the flames. What the hell was he doing? There was nothing important enough in that shed to risk his life for.

Her feet followed him anyway. She wasn't even conscious of deciding to do it—she just moved steadily closer to the shed. Heat blasted her body as a breeze gusted through the narrow passageway between the two buildings. It was functioning as a wind tunnel, funneling oxygen to the greedy fire.

Shouting to Xavier, she told him to concentrate the water on the wall closest to the main building. The shed was a complete loss, but hopefully they could contain the damage.

Ashes and tiny pieces of charred wood rained over her head and shoulders. Squinting her eyes against the heat and blazing light, Marcy tried to find Simon.

"Simon!"

He yelled at her. She thought he told her to get back, but she ignored him. Walking farther into the passageway between the buildings, she finally saw him through the haze of smoke. He was crouched close to the ground. She couldn't see what he was next to, but it was definitely a dark shape.

She almost yelled at him then. Until she saw the shape move and realized it was someone, not just something. Two someones. From the construction crew. One was stretched out on the ground, the other crouching behind Simon next to him.

The electrical box was only a few feet away. The man on the ground must have been the one shocked.

How had Simon known they were back here? By the time she'd arrived, the smoke had been too thick to see them.

Simon threw her a dark glance when she fell down beside him. She ignored it. He could be angry with her later when the fire was out and they knew the man would be fine.

She was relieved to see that his eyes were open and his chest was rising and falling steadily. Turning to her, Simon ordered her, "Go. We're right behind you." Scooping the man up into his arms, Simon waited until she and the other man were dashing ahead of him before following.

Marcy glanced back over her shoulder several times, just to make sure he was there. Even in a crouch, staying low to the ground where the smoke wasn't as thick and carrying a two-hundred-pound man, Simon could haul ass. Their little knot burst through the end of the passageway and the small group of people around them cheered.

The panic that had been almost palpable when they'd arrived eased. The flames licking at the shed had diminished. Three sides were now only smoldering, thick curls of smoke rolling up from the jagged edges of the damp wood. The fourth side would be joining them shortly if Xavier had anything to say about it.

Marcy was impressed with how he'd handled the crisis, and if she'd still been in charge would have offered him a raise on the spot. But she wasn't.

From his position on the hose, he hollered over to Simon, "MedFlight should be here shortly. How's he doing?"

Simon grunted and laid the man gently on the soft grass away from the smoke and flames. "Okay, but I'm not taking any chances."

Frowning, Simon looked up into the sky. As if he'd conjured them, the steady *thwap, thwap, thwap* of rotor blades joined the noise around them. Leaning over to one of the restaurant staff, he shouted something in her ear. With a nod, she burst out across the resort, directing the helicopter to the closest patch of open ground big enough for it to land.

Xavier kept the stream of water directed at the still-smoking building as the force of the downdraft pushed another burst of oxygen-rich air across the fire zone. Whether because of that or the daring glare that Xavier directed at the structure, the flames stayed down.

One man stooped low beneath the spinning blades

and dashed across the resort toward the cluster of people. A couple of bags were slung over his shoulders. The equipment looked as if it weighed a ton, but his body barely reacted to the stress of it.

Two more men followed behind, a stretcher between them. They crouched and worked, assessing and preparing the man for transport to the hospital. As they were getting ready to leave, one of them came over to Simon.

"We didn't get the call that there was a fire here, just the electrical shock. Do you need me to radio in for reinforcements from St. Lucia?"

Looking across at Xavier, Simon waited for a shake of his head before declining the offer. "I think we have it handled, but thanks."

With a nod, the man rushed after the rest of the crew. Once the stretcher was strapped in, the chopper lifted off. Marcy turned her face away from the tiny pieces of debris that lashed her.

Simon wrapped his arms around her and turned her so that her face was buried against his chest. Ducking his own head, he rested his cheek on her hair.

He smelled of soot and man. His shirt was damp, but she burrowed closer to him anyway. Her body started to shake. She knew it was just a delayed reaction to everything that had happened, her muscles revolting against the stress and the flood of adrenaline that was quickly receding.

But she couldn't stop it.

She wasn't cold. Not really. But her teeth began to chatter anyway.

Simon must have felt it, because he pulled away, holding her at arm's length as he looked at her. His eyes, intent and focused, studied her face. Without looking away he shouted, "Xavier, you got everything under control?"

"Yep, we're all good. Fire's out. I'll keep someone on watch through the night for hot spots, but I don't expect any."

"Great" was Simon's only response. With a sweep of his arms, he picked her up and cradled her against his body.

Marcy sputtered, but the protest she wanted to make died on her lips.

This was a side of Simon she'd never seen. One that intrigued and—if she was honest with herself— aroused her. Where was the laid-back surf god she'd been butting heads with for the past two years? Had he been kidnapped by tree sprites and held hostage in the jungle?

The man holding her in his arms was commanding, no-nonsense and completely capable. Not that that last one really surprised her. She'd always known a capable businessman lurked beneath that jovial, joking facade. That's what had frustrated her so much.

He could give a damn—he just chose not to. As far as she was concerned, that was a complete waste of his potential. And nothing bothered her more than to watch something useful go unused.

"Where are you taking me?" she asked, finally breaking the charged silence that had settled between them.

"Where do you think?" He bit out the words through stiff jaws.

He was upset. She thought she knew why but de- cided, in light of this new side to Simon, she wasn't going to act on the assumption. Probably better to wait for solid ground.

Turning sharply, he headed for the main entrance to the hotel. "To get cleaned up?" she said hopefully.

A humorless chuckle rumbled through his body. She could feel the vibrations of it roll through her like the reverberations from a plucked guitar string. They rekindled the burning need that the crisis had dampened.

Better than the teeth chattering.

Pushing through the front door, he let it slam behind them. The cool interior of the building was dark and a few steps inside only the weakest light remained. Outside, she realized, it was late afternoon, but inside it felt closer to dusk.

"No water, remember. And by the time we can stop pouring water over that building, chances are the reservoir will be dry."

Marcy cursed, but there wasn't any heat behind her words. Sure, a shower would be nice, but that would mean he'd have to put her down. She didn't want to examine too closely why that idea didn't appeal to her right now.

He strode through the building, heading for the stairs. Taking them two at a time, he began the climb up four flights. She could feel the powerful surge of his muscles as they bunched and moved beneath her.

Looking down at her arms tangled tightly around Simon's neck, she realized they were dirty. Dark patches of soot covered her upper arms. Trails of naked skin peeked through where stray drops of water had fallen and rolled down.

She was nasty.

Looking up into his face, she realized she wasn't the only one covered in soot. Streaks of it ran down over his forehead and cheeks. The sharp tang of burning wood clung to their skin.

He was filthy.

She didn't care.

The vision of him running beside that burning building burst through her mind. Another surge of adrenaline accompanied it.

Letting go with one hand, she used it to smack his shoulder.

Stopping midstride, his eyebrows crashing together, he said, "Ow! What was that for?"

They were halfway up, perched on the landing for the third floor. His voice echoed through the confined space, bouncing all around them.

"That was for being stupid and heading into the fire."

His expression cleared and a knowing grin twitched at the corners of his lips.

Continuing their climb, he argued, "I didn't head into the fire."

"Semantics. You were close enough to be burned. Or overcome by smoke inhalation. How did you know they were back there, anyway?"

"One of the crew told me when I arrived. At first they thought it was safer to leave him there until the helicopter came. But then the fire spread and the smoke shifted, cutting off the passageway. They were about to go in after them and I told them to wait."

"So that you could play hero yourself."

"Because I already had one man down, possibly two, that I was responsible for. I wasn't about to let two more follow."

Damn. She had seriously underestimated this man.

Something in the center of her chest swelled, but before she could analyze it, Simon was kicking open the stairway door to the top floor.

Anticipation, desire and apprehension swirled through her, a dangerous combination that was uncomfortable and energizing at the same time. She had no illusions as to why Simon was carrying her into his apartments. They'd started something in the jungle, and despite the interruption, he had every intention of following through and finishing it.

And if she wasn't sure about that she needed to decide now. Before he overwhelmed her senses again and logical thought became impossible.

She opened her mouth to say something, although she honestly wasn't sure what, but he cut her off.

"And while we're on the subject, what kind of incompetent work crew did you hire? First they break the main waterline. Then they get one of their men injured and start an electrical fire. Really, Marcy, is that what you call doing a good job?"

He stared down at her. Despite the fact that his eyes were hard and direct, she could still see the glimmer of passion lurking in the back.

"Excuse me? I'm damn good at my job."

Simon opened his door, then pushed it closed with the heel of his shoe behind them. Instead of moving straight to the bedroom as she'd expected, he stopped in the middle of his living room. Still holding her in his arms, he stood there.

Undercurrents flew between them, even as they continued their conversation. "Were. Were damn good at your job. You quit, remember?"

"Right." And that was an important thing to remember because the minute she gave in to whatever this was between them, the possibility of working for him again would be gone forever. After what had happened in New York, she refused to sleep with anyone she worked with—especially someone she worked *for*.

"The crew I usually use was unavailable until Friday. We had a long list and a short time to complete it. We needed a full crew for the entire two weeks. I couldn't wait for them. These guys came highly recommended."

"By who? The three stooges?"

"One of the men I usually use."

"I'm guessing these guys are blackmailing him for referrals, because I doubt they could figure out which end of a hammer to use."

Dropping her arms from around his neck, she crossed them over her chest. She didn't want to be impressed by the way he compensated for the loss of her help in keeping her rear end off the floor. But she couldn't help it.

His arm muscles bunched and his chest flexed. She could see the clearly defined bulge beneath the thin, wet material of his shirt. He was built. Why had she never noticed that before? Maybe she should take up surfing instead of running if the result was that kind of muscle tone.

"Give them some credit. They fixed the roof of the restaurant with no problems. Hammers aren't their issue. I will admit that perhaps plumbing and electrical jobs are out of their jurisdiction."

"I don't have to give them credit for anything. They've cost me enough money. I'm firing them."

"And how do you propose to finish the list of repairs and renovations before we reopen?"

He leaned over her, bringing their mouths centimeters apart. His eyes flared as they toured slowly across her face to settle on her mouth. They glittered with a promise and heat that sent awareness zinging through her body.

He hummed, deep in his throat. The sound was wild and sexy, a last warning of his intent.

"I guess that's my problem now. Last chance. If you want to walk out that door you better do it now, because in sixty seconds I won't be able to let you go."

It was the sexiest thing any man had ever said to her. What woman could resist that kind of naked admission?

Not her. Giving in was inevitable, but that didn't mean she had to throw all caution to the wind. Caution was part of her DNA.

"I'm not staying."

"I don't remember suggesting you would."

"I just want to make sure you know this won't change anything."

His mouth dropped to her throat and trailed across her skin. The sharp edge of his teeth followed the tendon that curved from her neck down her shoulder. He didn't hurt her, but it was hard to miss the implication that he could have…if he'd wanted to. That kind of leashed power was intoxicating.

His words brushed softly against her skin, but that did nothing to lessen their impact. "You're wrong. It's going to change a lot of things."

"But not me leaving," she breathed out, trying desperately to keep hold of her thoughts.

He lifted his head and speared her with his gaze. She felt hunted, vulnerable, desired.

"No, whatever this is won't keep you from leaving."

She dampened her dry lips, rolling them into her

mouth and swiping her tongue across them. "As long as we're clear."

"Oh, we're clear."

8

Simon stalked into the bedroom, her body tucked safely against his own.

He did not like the dirt that covered her skin. Not because it bothered him that she was dirty—it didn't—but because it meant she'd gotten close enough to the fire to be hurt.

When she'd materialized out of the smoke beside him in that tiny alley he'd wanted to growl and yell and carry her as far away from the danger as possible. Logically, he'd realized that wasn't possible. He'd needed to take care of the injured man. But at that moment logic had only barely come into play.

He moved to set her onto the dark navy bedspread covering the king-size mattress in the middle of the room. Marcy protested, a high-pitched squeak erupting from her. "Don't you dare. You'll ruin it. We're filthy."

"I don't care," he answered, dropping her onto the soft surface. He'd buy a new bed if he had to, but nothing was going to stop him from having her. Right now.

Marcy tried to keep her body off the comforter as she scrambled for the other side of the bed. She glared at him over her shoulder, but he didn't let that deter him. Grasping her by the ankle, he stopped her retreat and pulled her back to the center of the bed.

"Give it up. It's already dirty," he rumbled.

Marcy collapsed onto her stomach diagonally across his bed, her tangled hair running down her back. Without thought, he brushed the mass away, revealing the tender flesh at her nape. It was soft and fragrant as he buried his face against her. That tempting scent of hers clouded around him, overpowering the bitter smell of smoke. This was what he wanted. Something easy and beautiful to crowd out everything else.

His lips caressed her skin.

She made a small sound deep in her throat, something between a protest and anticipation. "Don't do that. I'm covered in soot."

"Not here," he whispered against her neck. He watched with fascination as goose bumps erupted across her skin. How could the rough texture of them against his mouth be this arousing?

He sucked a tiny taste of her into his mouth. Her back arched, pushing her closer against him. Breath caught in her lungs, the tiny hitch rocketing through him.

He wanted more.

Needed to see all of her, now. Pulling back, he grasped the neckline of her shirt and ripped.

"Don't—" she protested, but the threads were already coming apart in his hands. He wanted to see her that way, wild and ravaged as he pumped relentlessly inside her.

"I liked this shirt," she said with a resigned sigh. Ever practical, she wouldn't waste time fighting about something that couldn't be undone. Good for him, since the last thing he wanted to do was fight with her.

"It needed to be put out of its misery anyway. What? High school?"

"College."

His fingers slid down the exposed arch of her spine, a gentle caress that she bowed against. His fingers played beneath the string of the bikini top that circled her chest. Taking the ends, he tickled them over her skin, pulling a small moan of protest from her parted lips. Slowly he tugged at the tie until it finally let go.

His lips and fingers roamed. Her body was hot against his mouth. Her skin was soft and smooth, tempting him to take more. Even there, she had a tiny sprinkling of freckles and he paused long enough to pay homage to the few close by.

Darting his tongue out, he let it slide languidly over the tiny bumps of her spine. Her hips bucked when he reached the waistband of her shorts.

"For god's sake, take them off."

"If you insist," he said, a grin tugging at his lips.

She was as enflamed by this as he was. Knowing that only made the ache inside worse. He wanted to see the fire in her eyes as she finally broke apart beneath him. For two years he'd tried not to think about this moment, but had failed miserably.

Now he had the reality and it was so much better than anything even his imagination could have conjured up.

Marcy lifted her hips, sliding her hands beneath her to work the snap and zipper. She struggled, wiggling back and forth, and he just watched, enjoying the way her body undulated and the desperation that made her clumsy.

The waistband relaxed, slipping down and revealing the dent at the top of her ass. Without waiting for her to finish, he leaned over and ran his mouth along the newly exposed skin.

"Damn," she breathed out. Her body twisted beneath him, but with him pressed against her, she just couldn't get enough leverage to rid herself of the shorts and bathing-suit bottom.

Taking pity on them both, he curled his fingers in at her hips and pulled them off. She was beautiful.

Propped on her elbows, Marcy watched him over the curve of her shoulder. Her blue eyes smoldered, as hot as the fire they'd both just fought.

Without breaking their connection, Simon reached between her legs and pressed gently, asking her to spread wider for him. She did. The soft rasp of her thighs against the comforter as they opened for him rippled down his body.

His erection pressed painfully against his own zipper, but he wasn't about to let it free. Not yet. If he did, this would end way too soon. He wanted his fill of her first.

He ran his fingers softly up the insides of her thighs, just as he'd done when she was asleep. Only this time there was nothing to stop him from following all the way up to the soft pink center of her sex. Oh, and this time she watched him with half-lidded eyes, sharp arousal stamped on her face.

She rolled her hips, trying to hurry his journey upward, but he refused to rush. He tortured her, running his hands up and down her legs, over the curve of her ass, brushing as close to the center of her sex as possible without actually touching.

Every time he got close, Marcy's body jerked. The

response was involuntary. He knew without a doubt because he watched the warring emotions deep in her eyes—desperate need fought against a refusal to open her mouth and ask for what she wanted. It was silly, but it became a game of who would break first.

It wasn't the first time they'd played this particular game, although it was the first time they'd done it in bed. Simon had to admit this version was a hell of a lot more interesting and enjoyable.

And even if she couldn't reach him to effect a little physical torture of her own, Marcy was far from helpless. She had plenty of weapons at her disposal and had no problem using them.

Widening her legs even more, she exposed the swollen center of her sex. Simon growled, deep in his throat. She was slick, covered with the evidence of her arousal. For him. The scent of that arousal filled the air around him, making his heart pound restlessly in his chest and his fingers clamp hard around the tops of her thighs.

She rolled her hips, this time deliberately, hiding and then revealing what he really wanted. And he lost it. Without even touching him, she'd won.

He had to feel her, taste her, have her before he went mad.

Spreading the folds of her sex, he dived in and latched his mouth hard against her. She whimpered and bucked beneath him, just as devastated as he was. And that took some of the sting of his defeat away.

That and the taste of her on his tongue.

He lapped at her, enjoying her instant reaction when he brushed across the nub of her clit. He played there, relishing the way she panted, squirmed and ground harder against his mouth. His tongue speared inside her and the enveloping heat of her had a red-hot haze clouding everything, everything but her.

Somewhere in the back of his mind he realized he should probably stop, probably slow down and take a minute. But he didn't want to. Couldn't seem to find the will to do it. He'd never been this overwhelmed and out of control with a woman before in his life. He was a calculating lover. He knew exactly what to do, exactly where to touch, when to push and when to back off to give his partner the most explosive orgasm possible.

But he couldn't back off. Not this time. He wanted to feel her fall apart against his mouth. He wanted the pulse of her against his lips. He wanted the taste of her orgasm on his tongue.

Marcy arched her back, straining hard against him. She buried her head against the bed, muffling the sounds of her pleasure. But he even wanted that. He wanted everything she had and all she could give him.

Her body bowed tight beneath him, every single muscle straining for the release that he knew was so close. And when she finally gave in, her body convulsing and quivering with the force of it, he wasn't disappointed. She screamed, his name hot on her lips.

And he wanted more.

MARCY COLLAPSED onto the bed, her body trembling with the aftermath of spent desire.

Holy shit. But despite the satisfaction rolling through her body, she wasn't fulfilled. Just getting off wasn't enough. If that was all she'd wanted, she could have handled that herself. Although it definitely wouldn't have been anywhere close to as good as what Simon had just done to her. But still…she wasn't finished, and considering his fingers continued to roam across her skin, she didn't think he was, either.

He'd better not be.

Gathering her shaking legs beneath her, Marcy pushed up and rolled over. Luckily Simon was quick on the draw, because the electrical pulses running through her body had apparently impaired her control over her own muscles. Her leg flailed, her knee coming millimeters from colliding with his chin.

His palm cupped her leg, guiding it back down to the bed. He settled his mouth at the juncture where her thigh met her hip and sucked. She nearly came off the bed again, the sensation somehow tickling and driving her crazy at the same time.

But she wasn't about to let him drag her back under. Pushing against his head, Marcy sent him rocking back onto his heels between her spread thighs. Confusion pulled his eyebrows down over smoldering eyes.

A shiver took her, a combination of aftershock and the intensity of the unspent desire she saw in his eyes.

"Take 'em off," she ordered, pointing her finger from the tip of his head down to his toes so he knew she meant every last stitch.

She was sprawled out before him, completely naked. Had acted like a wanton hussy from the moment his hands touched her body. And she was tired of being vulnerable all alone.

Scooting away, he stood at the end of the bed. Marcy propped herself up on her elbows and settled in to enjoy the show. He crossed his arms over his body, grasped the edge of his shirt and lifted it up slowly. This wasn't the mundane task of taking off one piece of clothing so it could be replaced by another. It was so much more—the first time she would see all of him, everything he hid from the world beneath those careless clothes.

And right now she wanted that more than her next breath.

Hard abs appeared and her mouth began to water. She licked her lips. It was the closest she was getting to running her tongue across those valleys and planes—at least for now.

His skin was bronzed by the sun. A light dusting of blond hair curled over the swell of his pecs, narrowing and disappearing beneath the band of his shorts.

He pulled his head through the opening of his shirt. His blond hair clouded out around his head in sexy disarray. The shirt was ruined, dirt, soot and water ground into the fibers. For the first time, Marcy noticed the singed edges and a renewed blast of fear settled heavily in her chest.

Simon could have been seriously hurt.

But he hadn't been. Studiously pushing the unwelcome and unproductive thought from her mind, she focused all her attention on the amazing body he was revealing.

Strong fingers popped the button at the top of his fly and then deliberately tugged at the tab of his zipper. The sound of metal grinding against metal filled the room and her legs scissored restlessly against the bed.

He rolled his hips and the khaki shorts hit the floor. Beneath them the tantalizing length of his erection strained against confining briefs. Red. She should have known there was nothing plain about this man. Everything about him was bold and unapologetic.

And while that bugged the crap out of her in their business dealings, she had to admit that in bed it was sexy as hell.

He knew what he wanted and he took it. Today, right now, he wanted her, and she had no problems with that.

Pushing up onto her knees, Marcy crawled to the end of the bed and knelt in front of him. Her palms bracketed his hips. The heat of him exploded through her, stealing what little breath she had left. She half expected him to take over again, to kiss her and bend her backward beneath him. But he didn't.

Moving her hands up his chest, she enjoyed the way the soft hair tickled her palms. The sharp intake of breath through his teeth as she grazed the sensitive peak of a nipple reverberated through her body. Her breasts tingled, feeling neglected.

He reached for her then, taking the sharp peaks between thumb and finger and rolling gently. She elongated the curve of her spine, pressing the aching tips harder into his hold.

Leaning into his body, she brought their mouths together and whispered, "I thought I said to take it all off."

His sharp eyes flashed, deep and fierce. "I'm a little busy. Why don't you do it?"

He continued to play with her breasts, pinching, tugging and driving her crazy before taking the soft center of his palm and rubbing in gentle circles, easing some of the ache. He did it over and over again, sending spikes of need shooting through her body straight to her sex. Arouse, relieve, arouse, relieve. The cycle was maddening.

She did what he asked, but only because it was what she wanted, too. Marcy cupped her palm around the hard length straining against the red-hot fabric. Simon groaned deep in his throat. Slipping her hand beneath the imprisoning waistband, she found him hot and hard, and squeezed.

Closing her eyes, she relished the feel of him. All silky-smooth skin, burning heat and pulsing veins, filling her palm and spilling over. She couldn't even spread her fingers and touch all of him.

"Damn, you've been hiding a lot more than killer abs beneath those rumpled clothes you like so much."

He laughed, a low rumble. And thrust his hips, pushing his length harder against her palm. A thrill raced down her spine at the thought of him buried deep inside her, filling her up and stretching her as far as she could go.

"If I'd known you were going to be this impressed I'd have shown you mine a long time ago."

"Egomaniac," she answered, even as she slid up and down, trying to memorize every inch of him.

He let her play. Somewhere along the way she managed to remove his briefs so that she could see everything she had in her hand. She devoured him with her eyes. Her tongue licked across her lips and he bucked in the tight confines of her hold.

Her fingers slipped through the evidence of his arousal, taking the clear liquid and spreading it around the sensitive head. His hips rocked with her caresses, soft at first but quickly moving faster and faster. An answering frenzy built inside her.

With hard purpose, he claimed her mouth. She tasted that same frenzy on his lips and thrilled to it. His hands were all over her, everywhere at once. And she couldn't get enough.

As he pushed her backward with the force of his kiss, she could do nothing but let him follow her down and hope that she came out the other side of this experience unscathed.

Her fingers curled into his hard hips, holding on. His body rubbed against her, all of her skin tingling beneath the caress. A whimper of anticipation slipped through her lips.

He reached above her, yanked open the bedside table, pulled out a condom and didn't bother closing the drawer again as he ripped into the foil with his teeth. Before she could process what he was doing the condom was over his erection.

Her mouth was dry. Her sex wet. Her body on fire with an aching need. It had been so long since she'd felt this way. Alive. Sensual. Wanted.

Grasping her hips, Simon pulled her back to him. Wrapping an arm beneath her knee, he crushed her leg up and opened her wide for whatever he wanted. Cold air mixed with the heat of desire and she whimpered. She was empty and she wanted him to fill her.

"Simon. Now. Please," she begged.

He speared her with a dark gaze and then with slow, sure strokes, invaded her in the best possible way. Her internal muscles protested for the space of a heartbeat before stretching around him, taking everything he'd given her.

She wanted more. He was holding back. She could see it in the concentrated strain of his face and feel it in the quiver of his muscles. Looking down at where their bodies joined, she realized he had inches left to give her. She was greedy and wanted it all.

Pulling her hips wider, she opened for him. And burying her heels into his flanks, Marcy urged him on. He resisted, pushing against her.

"I don't want to hurt you," he gritted out through straining jaws.

She clenched her internal muscles. He hissed.

"You won't," she promised, even as she surged beneath him, lifting her hips and taking all of him. He slid home, burying himself inside her to the hilt.

He hissed again. His eyes glazed over with mindless passion. Breath panted through his still-clenched teeth and his ribs contracted and expanded beneath her hands, like the flanks of a horse that had just run hell-for-leather. He was trying desperately to cling to sanity and control. Only, she didn't want him to.

She tried every trick she knew to get him to let go—undulating against him, reaching between their joined bodies to caress his tight balls, contracting her sex around him—but he wasn't giving in. He stayed there, not moving, driving her crazy.

And while she'd gotten exactly what she wanted—all of him—it left her with little space to maneuver. But, God, the hot, hard feel of him deep inside her was worth the price.

After several seconds the haze lifted and he looked deep into her, blue eyes clear and blistering. She trembled under the intensity of that gaze.

"Minx," he breathed, the soft caress against her skin jolting deep inside her. She was so close to the edge of losing it.

He pumped slowly against her, pulling out and thrusting back in. This time he didn't hold anything back. Each time he left her empty she thought she would scream, only to have him fill her so completely she wasn't sure she could ever live without the sensation again.

Her hips gyrated beneath him, meeting him thrust

for thrust, urging him higher, harder, faster. The bed trembled, and somewhere in the back of her mind she worried they'd ruin it right along with the linens.

But it would be so worth it.

She wanted this moment to last forever, to teeter on the amazing edge he'd driven them both to. But it couldn't. The consolation was that Simon broke at the same time, both of them coming together. His hips surged against her, hard. Every muscle in her body responded, contracting and pulsing and quivering.

Her cries mingled with his shouts and Marcy was grateful they were entirely alone in the large hotel. Because if anyone else had been in the place they would have heard, floors and walls be damned.

Simon collapsed beside her, half on and half off, their bodies still joined. It wasn't something that Marcy usually liked. Aside from the idea of being crushed beneath some big male body that most likely was a foot taller and fifty pounds heavier than she was, she just didn't like feeling trapped.

But she didn't mind it at all with Simon. In fact, if he'd tried to move, she probably would have protested. The weight of him against her felt like the only thing keeping her together. And the solid feel of him still inside her was reassuring as aftershock after aftershock rolled through her.

Eventually Simon pulled away. Rolling onto his back, he tucked her against him. His skin was warm under her cheek. The steady thrum of his heart was hypnotic, and exhaustion filled her. Her eyelids fluttered closed. She'd just rest for a few minutes.

Her next conscious thought was that something was tickling her hip. She swatted at it…and her fingers got tangled with Simon's. Her eyes flew open.

Moonlight filled the room.

"How long have I been asleep?" she asked, her voice still rough with sleep.

"Awhile," Simon answered. He had levered himself onto one elbow and was looking down at her, a tempting light in his eyes. She knew she probably looked awful. Her skin was no doubt flushed red, her hair a mess and soot most likely still coated her arms and legs.

He reached over to place a kiss on the curve of her shoulder and she shied away.

She didn't like his frown as he asked, "Why'd you pull away?"

"I'm still dirty," she said, lips curling up in distaste.

His frown cleared and a soft chuckle escaped. The urge to reach up and kiss him rolled through her, but she didn't give in to it. She was on shaky ground here, and didn't know what he'd consider acceptable lover behavior.

"Is that all? Most of it rubbed off on the comforter."

Marcy looked down at her arms and realized he was right. "Oh, and that makes it so much better."

The soot was mostly gone, only a few minuscule streaks left here and there. But she could still feel it on her skin. "I really wish the water was working. I'd kill for a shower."

Simon trailed a single finger down the center of her body, going through the valley between her breasts and circling lazily around her belly button.

"I don't think killing is the answer, Ms. McKinney. But I might have a solution?"

"Oh yeah, what's that?" she asked, trying desperately to keep hold of the thread of the conversation.

How could his simple, playful touch—after she'd just come twice—arouse her again so quickly?

He clicked his tongue in an admonishing sound. "What's it worth to you?"

"What do you mean?"

"Well, you were willing to kill for a shower a few minutes ago. What's my solution worth to you?"

Marcy's eyes narrowed, even as a smile touched her lips. Her fingers found their way to the nape of his neck and began playing there, twisting the strands lazily through them.

"Well, the inherent value is less because I'm purchasing an unknown."

"I promise it will accomplish the same goal as a shower."

She shrugged, the muscles of her stomach leaping beneath his touch. "I'm not in the habit of taking charming men at their word."

"Been burned a time or two?"

"Maybe."

Leaning over her, he claimed her mouth in a kiss that held every bit as much passion as the kiss in the jungle—the one that had sent them here. The only difference was this time there was a familiarity that set her a little on edge. It was nice. But it also scared her. It would be so easy to fall under the spell of this charming, gallant man. At least when he was treating her as if she were precious and unique.

"Grab a shirt out of the closet," he said, pulling back. "We'll settle on payment later."

9

DIGGING IN THE BOTTOM of a drawer, Simon pulled out some gray pajama bottoms that had never been worn. He couldn't even remember why they were there since he always slept nude, but it didn't matter.

Turning around, he was just in time to watch as Marcy pulled an old college T-shirt over her head. The sight of her covering her body shouldn't have been sexy, but it was. The hem of the faded navy fabric brushed over her skin, falling to settle halfway down her thighs. Considering he was so tall and she was so short, it more than covered the important bits. But he knew what waited underneath.

And he had every intention of seeing it again. Tonight.

Grabbing her hand, he pulled her out of his apartments and through the hotel. Their bare feet pattered softly against the stairs.

Every few feet they passed beneath the red circle of an emergency light, but in between they were surrounded by darkness. He could barely see her in the

blackness. There were windows in the stairwell, but it
was the middle of the night.

They burst onto the first floor of the hotel. Here soft
moonlight fell through the wide windows fronting the
lobby, gilding everything in silver. A shadowy figure
moved silently through the space ahead of them. Simon
stopped, and with the connection of their joined hands,
pulled Marcy in close behind him.

There might be more light here, but it wasn't enough
to tell who was in front of them. The figure was tall
and lean and, Simon decided, male. Although his
shoulders were slightly slumped. The initial burst of
surprise and concern eased—definitely not a defensive
or antagonistic posture.

And when the figure said, "Simon," he felt all the
tension leave his body.

"Xavier."

"I was just coming to find you."

He wanted to say, *What now?* But one look at the
exhaustion on Xavier's face as he walked through a
brighter patch of light had the words dying on his lips.
"You look awful, man."

His lips twisted. "Thanks."

Marcy stepped from behind Simon, pulling her hand
out of his in the process. He let her go, although something deep inside gave a silent growl and urged him to
grab her back. He ignored it.

Tugging self-consciously at the hem of the shirt,
Marcy asked, "What's wrong?"

"Nothing. Nothing." Xavier ran his hand through
his hair, ruffling the dark brown mess, which was still
wet. All he managed to do was stand it on end, making
him resemble a porcupine.

"I wanted to give you an update before I grab some

sleep. Paul and Christine are patrolling the site of the fire, although I wouldn't expect any flare-ups. There's enough water on the sucker that you could advertise you now have a mud bath available."

They all chuckled softly.

"Any news on the guy they took out by MedFlight?" Frowning, Simon asked, "Anyone even know his name?"

Marcy bit her lip, drawing Simon's attention. He pulled his gaze away—now wasn't the time.

"I didn't get all of their names, but the leader's name is Jake," she said.

Xavier nodded. "I spoke to Jake. The injured worker's wife met the chopper at the hospital. He appears fine. They're keeping him overnight for observation, but so far no adverse effects."

"Wonderful." Simon sighed with relief.

The guy might have been trying to take on a project he didn't have the experience to tackle, but that didn't mean Simon wanted him to pay permanently for that bad decision. He didn't want anyone hurt on his watch.

He reached out and clamped a hand on Xavier's shoulder. "Excellent work. That was a real baptism by fire, and it could have been much worse without your quick thinking and strong leadership. I don't believe I've ever given anyone a raise in their first week, but I'm all for breaking the rules. See me tomorrow and we'll talk."

Xavier nodded, not even really responding to the praise Simon had just heaped on his head. Not that Simon blamed him. It was obvious he was running on empty.

"Get some sleep," he said, squeezing Xavier's shoulder before letting go.

Simon and Marcy stood silently, watching him as he turned and walked back out of the building.

"He deserves every penny that you're going to give him," Marcy said.

Looking down at her, he realized they stood shoulder to...well, her head. He grasped her hand in his again. Turning, she looked up into his face.

"Now, you promised me something equivalent to a shower." She raised a single eyebrow—question, dare, invitation.

Raising one of his own, he paused long enough to claim her lips before leading her through the lobby and out into the night. It was so quiet, even the ever-present sound of crashing waves seemed muted.

It didn't take them long to reach the pool complex. Usually surrounded by laughing people, it was now empty. Well-placed vegetation gave the area a sense of privacy that Simon knew was an illusion—one he'd conjured on purpose. Even the concrete shell for the showers and changing rooms at the far end of the pool was camouflaged with brightly colored flowers and lush green bushes.

The water was calm and clear, inviting.

"No way," Marcy said, tugging softly against his hold on her hand. She tried to walk backward, pulling him with her. She didn't get far, only the length of their fully outstretched arms.

"What do you mean, no way?"

"I am not swimming naked in a public pool." Spearing him with her gaze, she said, "That is what you had in mind right, considering neither of us has a bathing suit?"

"Well, I suppose you could swim in my shirt, if you really want." His eyes toured slowly down Marcy's body.

This time he knew exactly what waited for him under the material of her clothing—lush curves and soft skin. Immeasurable pleasure. Maybe it was a good thing she'd always worn those nondescript, boxy business suits around him, because if he'd known earlier what was hidden beneath… Yeah, it wouldn't have taken him two years to get a taste, that was for sure.

Her skin flushed, but her eyes sharpened. "Please."

He'd seen that expression more times than he cared to count. It was her stubborn, taking-a-stance-and-not-gonna-budge expression. They'd just have to see about that.

"Do you think I'm stupid? You've already ripped one shirt. The minute I get in that water this one's toast."

His lips twitched. "I ripped *your* shirt. I happen to like that one." He gestured at it with their joined hands. "I have no intention of ruining it."

"So if I get in that pool, you promise not to try and get this shirt off me?"

"I didn't say that."

"That's what I thought."

She tugged again at their joined hands. Instead of letting her go, he jerked on the hold and used the momentum of her surprise. She stumbled against him and, lightning quick, he had his arms wrapped tightly around her, crushing their bodies together.

That scent, the one that was now entirely hers, enveloped him. He could feel the speeding thrum of her heart against his chest. Probably could've kissed her and convinced her to do whatever he wanted, but that would backfire on him later when it was all over and her temper flared.

Instead, he cajoled with words. "Everyone's asleep."

"Except for Paul and Christine."

"They're on the opposite side of the hotel. They can't see us from here. Hell, they can't even hear us. You know you want to, Marcy. For once in your life walk on the wild side."

"I walk on the wild side plenty," she countered, her nose wrinkling cutely as she frowned.

"Please. You don't know the meaning of the word *wild*. I've never met anyone as structured and uptight in my life."

She sputtered. He enjoyed seeing her at a complete loss for words. It didn't happen often.

"I am not uptight."

"Look, I don't have a problem with you being uptight. Actually, I like it. Makes you an easy target. But sometimes you need a little balance."

"Balance? That's rich coming from the man who divides his time between various entertaining activities without a spare moment left over for actual work."

A pang of guilt shot through the center of his chest. In all the time they'd known each other, Simon hadn't thought twice about the secret he was keeping from Marcy. He'd ignored her, dismissed her and outright lied to her without blinking an eye.

And he'd had good reasons.

Now they didn't seem so important. Part of him wanted to tell her the truth, but he couldn't do that. The tiny voice in his head told him he could trust Marcy. But then, he'd thought the same thing about Courtney.

He wouldn't make the same mistake twice. Not even because of stellar sex.

Truthfully, the stellar sex made him question the urge even more. Until right now, he'd never felt the need to tell her. So he'd keep his mouth shut…at least until he was sure any decision he made wasn't clouded by some misplaced afterglow effects.

Besides, he knew Marcy well enough to realize she would not appreciate learning he'd been lying to her for two years. And he wasn't ready to put that wedge between them.

Not when she was going to leave anyway. Yet another reason to keep his secret to himself.

"Sounds like I'm the perfect person to teach you something about being wild and irresponsible."

Scooping her up into his arms, Simon barely paused before stepping off the edge of the pool and plunging them both into the water. They were near the center, so the water only came to his waist. However, it completely soaked his pants, plastering the thin fabric to his body.

In her cradled position against his chest, Marcy barely got wet. In fact, only the back of his T-shirt was damp, water soaking slowly up from the bottom hem.

"Hold your breath," he warned right before opening his arms and letting her drop.

Aside from the sharp intake of breath, she didn't make a sound. Her body splashed into the water...and slowly sank.

He'd expected her to flail, or pop up quickly. He watched for several seconds, the navy cloud of shirt billowing around her until she settled on the bottom near his feet. Her body collapsed in slow motion, her hair floating around her head.

Simon panicked. What the hell? Bending his knees, he sank down and grasped a handful of shirt so that he could jerk her back up again.

Later, when he looked back on the moment, he

couldn't be sure exactly how it all happened. One minute he was hauling Marcy out of the water, afraid she was drowning, not understanding how that could happen since the water was shallow enough for her to stand.

The next, his feet had been swept out from under him. Already off balance, he went completely under. Water poured into his open mouth, but instinct had him spitting it out and holding his breath.

He opened his eyes beneath the water, trying to find his bearings and figure out what was going on. And Marcy was there, bubbles escaping slowly to drift around her face. Her eyes were open, too. Staring at him, a taunting smile curling her lips.

Before he could reach out and grab her, she darted away through the water, sleek as a seal.

The peal of her laughter hit him hard as he broke through the surface. The wet, clinging fabric of his pants slowed him down. Taking a few precious seconds, Simon jerked them off, leaving them to settle on the bottom of the pool in a gray blob.

The water was pleasant against his skin as he shot after her. She dived again, disappearing into the deep end. Although the trailing dark blue tail of his shirt was as good as a red flag.

She surfaced for air and he caught her. Beneath the water, his fingers slid over her soft skin. The force of her rocketing ascent piled his shirt high on her torso. It was nothing for him to grab it and pull it off her. He dropped it back into the water, and they watched together as it sank to the bottom.

His mouth latched onto the curve of her shoulder. Her skin tasted of chlorine and lavender. The broken surface of the water lapped gently around the curve of her breasts. The soft pink center of her nipples jutted temptingly.

She kicked her legs lazily, churning the water around them. The currents were like a caress.

"See, the wild side's not so bad, is it?" he whispered as he lapped droplets from the line of her collarbone.

She sighed, the soft gust of breath tickling his ear. "Too early to tell."

He wrapped his hands around her waist, holding her still as he ducked under the water. His eyes opened so that he could see her, the sting of chlorine worth every second. He took the distended bud of her nipple into his mouth. Her gasp was muffled, but he could feel the vibration of it against his fingers still splayed over her rib cage.

He rolled his tongue lazily around the hard nub before switching to the other side. Her skin was silky smooth and cool, unlike the heat building inside him. His lungs burned with the need for oxygen, but he wasn't ready to let her go. He wanted to stay there forever, lavishing her breasts with attention. Beneath the water, everything was muted and it felt as if there was nothing else in the world but the two of them.

Eventually he had to come up.

And when he did Marcy was there to meet him. Pushing her fingers into his wet hair, she dragged him up to her mouth and devoured him. The taste of her desire exploded against his lips. She didn't even let him wipe the water from his face, instead letting it rain down over both of them.

Droplets clung to her eyelashes, tiny glittering diamonds in the moonlight. Her legs floated up around him, bringing their bodies tight together. The heat of her center slid against his pounding erection.

Reaching down, he spread her open wider. His fingers slipped through the evidence of her desire, thicker than the water that tried to wash it away. She gasped, jerking tighter against him when he found and teased the swollen button of her clit.

He'd meant to bring them closer together, to tease them both, but he couldn't do it. Not now that he'd touched her. Sliding his fingers into her white-hot depths was inevitable.

He pushed one inside, and then another. Her muscles pulsed around his invasion. The same rhythm echoed deep inside, hammering through his blood. This need for her had somehow become a part of him, melding with the pieces that fit together to make him the man he was. Something that had never happened with another woman.

Marcy's head flew back. She clung to him, the water holding them both up. Her breath was fast. She trembled. He worked her, letting his fingers move in and out.

She was wild. So slippery that without her arms and legs clinging to him it would have been difficult to hold on.

Raising her head, she speared him with her gaze. Her eyes smoldered, hotter than her body wrapped so tightly around him. She licked her lips and said, "Please tell me you have a condom stashed somewhere."

Simon stilled. And groaned, a sound that had almost nothing to do with the fist she'd just wrapped around his cock.

"In my pants."

"Thank you," she breathed, looking up to the sky. Her fingers drifted lower, began to caress the heavy orbs hanging from his body. He really hated to stop her, but…

"At the bottom of the pool."

This time they both stilled. He could count her pulse by the throbbing beat at the center of her body where his hand was still buried deep. Her grip on him tightened somewhere just this side of painful. Together, they slowly turned their heads toward the shallow end.

Marcy laughed, a low, aching, sexy sound that rolled through him. Pushing away, she disentangled their bodies. He realized she was putting space between them to thwart temptation. But the primitive animal that had somehow inhabited his body wanted to howl a protest and haul her back to him.

"Which one of us is going down after it?"

"What you really mean is you're the idiot who let the condom sink to the bottom of the pool, so get your ass down there."

Her eyes glowed. It was different from the smoldering desire that had been there moments before. Although that glitter was still there, too. But now there was more. An…ease that had never been between them before.

"Since you put it that way."

Taking a deep breath, Simon dived, then pulled the soft cotton back up behind him. Slipping his hand into the pocket, he retrieved one of the tiny, important foil packets. Holding it up triumphantly, he turned to Marcy. Water dripped, landing noisily on the surface of the pool.

She frowned. It wasn't exactly the response he'd been hoping for.

"What's wrong?" he asked.

"Nothing." She shook her head. "I'm just trying to

remember everything I've read about water and con-
doms. Does a good soaking weaken the integrity?"

He stared at her. Seriously. "Weaken the integrity?
Jesus, Marcy, who talks like that?" Were they really
having this conversation? In the middle of the pool.
Naked.

While his body burned with a need for her.

Even floating in the deep end, with her feet nowhere
close to a solid surface, she somehow managed to place
her hands on her hips, cock her head to the side and
give him that "Marcy stance." He'd long ago realized
fighting her in this mood was like bashing his head
against a brick wall—he was the only one who ended
up in pain.

Ripping into it, he held up the perfectly dry condom.
"Dry as the desert."

Her eyes flashed and she crossed her arms over
her chest. He was absolutely sure she had no idea of
the effect. The edge of the water lapped tantalizingly
against her protruding nipples. His stomach muscles
clenched hard and beneath the surface his cock jerked
painfully toward her.

"Yeah, but for how long?"

"Huh?" he asked, unable to follow the conversation.
Not while fantasizing about what he was going to do to
her. Glancing behind him, he imagined her stretched
out beneath him across the gleaming white steps leading out of the pool.

"Dry. How long is it going to stay dry? In the pool."
She gestured offhandedly to his completely submerged
groin.

Surging toward her, he grasped her around the
waist and pulled her hard against him. "I don't care,"

he growled. "All I know is if I don't get inside you now I'm going to explode."

She looked up at him. Innocence mixed with mischief, a complicated combination that set him off-kilter. "Isn't that kinda the point?"

Had she just made a joke? He didn't think he'd ever heard Marcy do that.

Picking her up, he fought the pressure of the water, walking to the steps where he'd envisioned her just moments before. She didn't protest. Instead, when he laid her out on the wide ledge several steps up she stretched, undulating her body.

The shrewd look in her eyes told him she knew exactly what she was doing. And that was sexy as hell. He'd always been a sucker for a powerful, self-confident woman. And there was no one more confident in her own skin than Marcy.

Water lapped softly against her body, submerging her legs from the knee down. The waves they'd created in the empty pool teased against her hair, swirling it around her head one minute and leaving wet fingers of it trailing down the stairs the next.

The water reached just above his knees, but left the rest of him blessedly free. Somehow the condom had miraculously remained dry and he rolled it quickly down his pounding erection.

She watched his every move, those intelligent eyes missing nothing. Reaching out, she trailed a single fingertip down the latex-covered length. A strangled sound erupted from him, the combination of constricting latex and throbbing desire almost too much to bear.

"Satisfied?" he asked.

Marcy spread her thighs before him. Water caressed

the swollen pink slit of her sex. He wanted to be there. Doing that to her instead.

"If you mean am I satisfied that the condom is dry and not going to break, yes. If you mean am I satisfied with *you*—" her eyes flicked up to his before settling back on his erection "—I never thought you were the kind of man who fished for compliments. Does your ego need stroking?"

He growled deep in his throat. "No, but I damn sure know something that does."

She laughed, the tinkle of the sound settling somewhere in the middle of his chest and burrowing there. It itched and pinched and warmed him with a pleasant ache that had nothing to do with the fact that she was naked in front of him.

Reaching for him, she pulled him down on top of her. For a minute he worried about grinding her into the edge of the stairs, but the moment she wrapped her hand around him and guided him to the entrance of her body he forgot all about it. She didn't seem to mind.

He slid home inside her in one easy stroke. She arched beneath him, pushing their bodies tighter together and taking all of him.

Wrapping her arms around his neck, she held on tight. Each time he pushed high and hard against her, tiny bursts of air tickled his ear. They urged him on.

And so did her words. "You feel perfect inside me," she groaned as he pushed them both relentlessly to the edge. His body strained. His muscles shook. And she was with him every step of the way.

Her teeth latched onto his shoulder, holding on. Her labored breaths puffed against his skin. Every muscle in her body drew tight beneath him, a taut bow just waiting to snap. He relentlessly pushed them both, driving into her over and over.

Their bodies slapped together. Water rocked violently around them.

Marcy let go of him, falling back against the stair. With her eyes closed in ecstasy, her mouth opened wide on a silent cry that didn't, couldn't last.

She fell apart in his arms, bucking, writhing, a scream finally rolling up through her body, erupting at the top of her lungs.

Seeing her wild was an experience he'd never forget.

And he let himself fall behind her. A fiery ball of heat built at the center of his spine, exploding out to engulf all of him. His hips surged. The ravenous need that had built inside him spilled out and into her, his own guttural cry mixing with her scream.

He couldn't breathe. It felt as if he was down in the deep end again, his lungs straining, drowning in her. And just like then, he didn't care.

He might have stayed there forever, their legs and arms tangled together and his body buried deep inside her.

Except a voice interrupted the moment.

"What the heck was that?"

He recognized Paul's deep voice.

And Christine's higher one. "Don't you mean who? Sounded like sex to me."

"Maybe it was a jaguar?"

"That was no jaguar."

Marcy stirred beneath him. Still connected, their hips ground together and her breasts brushed his chest. Her body was tense, not from unspent desire but from the realization that their privacy was about to be invaded. And he had no doubt she did not want to be found stretched out naked on the stairs of the pool. With him.

Some perverse voice in his head suggested he should stay right where he was, let Paul and Christine find them like this so everyone on the island would know she was his. But that would be stupid. And definitely not what she'd want.

Simon gathered his spent body beneath him, meaning to roll away from her and provide a distraction if necessary so she could escape.

He was surprised when she reached up and stopped him. Her eyes hot and intense, she looked him straight in the eye and whispered, "Hell, yes, I'm satisfied."

He knew she didn't mean anything other than the face value of the words. But that didn't stop male pride from mixing with the buzz of satisfaction in his blood.

Scooping her up, he paid no attention to the water that rained down both of their bodies. Striding across the complex, he didn't stop until the door to the main building closed behind them. Everything was dark and silent. Marcy squirmed in his arms, silently ordering him to let her down.

He ignored her. He dragged his finger over her swollen bottom lip and said, "Of course you are. Your satisfaction almost got us caught."

_10_

SHE WAS MORTIFIED. Although she fought the urge to cover her tingling cheeks with her hands. She twisted harder against Simon's hold and he eventually put her feet to the floor. It was cool against her skin and for the first time she realized she was completely naked.

Yes, it seemed like a silly revelation considering what they'd just done. Twice. But she couldn't help it. She wasn't in the habit of running around public places without a stitch of clothing on.

Even if the guy she was with owned the place. Or maybe especially since the guy who owned it was with her.

She watched Simon. His blond hair was dark, flopping into his eyes. Where was the lazy man she'd worked with for the past two years? Somewhere over the past two days he'd disappeared, to be replaced by the man before her. Even the line of his jaw somehow seemed tighter, stronger.

Droplets of water rolled lazily down his chest to pool on the floor at his feet. She really should clean that up.

She'd thought she knew Simon. Apparently she was wrong. She'd believed the same thing about her old boss, as well. Dread twisted in the pit of her stomach. Marcy pushed it away. She didn't work for him anymore. She was not making the same mistake. Simon wasn't married. Was he?

"You don't have a wife tucked away somewhere, do you?"

Simon's eyes widened with shock, before narrowing slightly. He studied her for several silent seconds before finally answering. Or not answering. "I think that's the stupidest thing you've ever said to me."

Yeah, she knew she was being an idiot. But she couldn't help herself. Spinning to hide the embarrassed flush on her cheeks, Marcy disappeared behind the check-in desk and returned with several towels. She'd stopped long enough to wrap one around her sarong-style.

Silently she handed one to Simon. He rubbed it over his hair before slinging it haphazardly around his neck.

Shaking her head, Marcy crouched down and began mopping up the mess they'd left on the wooden floor. It would be ruined if they didn't get rid of the water.

She didn't get far. Simon reached beneath her arms and pulled her back up. Spinning her to face him, he drilled into her with his gaze and she thought maybe he saw more than she'd realized. It definitely felt as if he could see straight into her soul. She didn't like that at all. She had plenty of secrets she wanted to keep.

"What was that about?"

She opened her mouth, but closed it again before actually saying anything.

He waited. Not pushing her. Not wheedling for an answer that she was obviously reluctant to give. He didn't try to charm her or belittle the seriousness of the situation. He just calmly stood there, waiting.

And that's why she told him. "I dated a married man."

This time it was her turn to wait for the condemnation that usually came…that she deserved. But it didn't come.

"I didn't know he was married."

Simon nodded his head once, succinctly, as if that was all there was to say about the situation. As if her lack of knowledge was a given.

"It, um…" She cleared her throat nervously and hated herself for the show of weakness. "He was my boss."

Simon's jaw clenched. "He took advantage of you."

She laughed, a broken sound that gurgled up from deep inside her chest. "Hardly. Do I look like the kind of woman who'd let herself be taken advantage of?"

"At the moment?" His hand cupped the back of her head and his thumb skimmed softly down the side of her neck. The caress was different from the rest. Oh, the sizzle was there, but it was muted, overlaid by an understanding that surprised and humbled her.

She shook her head, not wanting him to say anything else that could make her care about him more than she already did. It was bad enough as it was, this connection she was suddenly allowed to explore.

"You look like a woman who's been hurt. And that makes you more human and accessible than all of your skill and competence and order."

A lump rose in her throat. She swallowed it, conscious of the way his thumb continued to stroke her skin.

"Accessible is overrated."

"So is being alone."

He pressed his lips to hers, a soft brush of skin to skin. And asked, "Do you think you're the only person who's ever been hurt?" against her mouth.

She tried to look at him, but he changed the angle of their kiss so that she couldn't see his eyes. She wanted to see the honesty there. To know the truth.

When he wouldn't give it to her, she pulled back again and asked him point-blank. "You've been hurt?"

She found the idea laughable. Simon Reeves, charming, sexy, roguish. He epitomized one-night stand. Although she had to admit that she'd never actually seen him take a lover from the many guests who'd thrown themselves at him during her time here.

But that didn't mean he'd had no meaningless affairs. It just meant he didn't poach from his own backyard.

She tried to imagine the man standing before her, unapologetically naked, going two years without a lover and almost laughed out loud.

He must have seen the suppressed flicker in her eyes. "What's so funny?"

"Nothing."

While she tried desperately not to dissolve into fits of laughter, his eyebrows slammed together.

"Fine, I was trying to remember the last time I'd seen you with a woman and couldn't come up with one since I've been here. And then I wondered if maybe you've been without one for the past two years. And that thought was funny as hell."

"I'm glad my dry spell in the bedroom could entertain you."

"Please," she said, finally giving in to the bubble floating through her chest.

He wrapped his hands around her waist and jerked her hard against him. His mouth settled roughly over hers. Heat suffused her, only this time it had nothing to do with embarrassment. She went under easily, dragged there by Simon's overwhelming need for her.

It felt as if his fingers burned through the cotton to brand her skin beneath. He let her go. She gasped. Her towel dropped heedlessly to the floor.

"That's exactly what I'm telling you. I haven't slept with a single woman since you stepped foot on this island."

She stared at him, dumbfounded. Her mouth went dry. She searched his face for some sign that he was lying. Or joking. Or playing one of his games.

But he wasn't. He was serious as a heart attack.

Something pinched sharply in the center of her chest.

He reached for her again, pulling her back into his arms, and she let him.

This time when his mouth claimed hers the aggression of a moment before was gone. Replaced by something else, something softer and more persuasive.

"Not laughing now, are you?"

SIMON STARED at the ceiling. It was still dark out, probably somewhere between two and three in the morning if he had to guess. And he couldn't sleep.

Beside him, Marcy breathed softly and evenly. She'd been out for at least two hours. And he couldn't blame her. He couldn't remember a time in his life when he'd come so many times. Not even during his wild college days. His reputation had been legendary, all of his part-

ners more than satisfied. But one or two rounds a night
had been his limit.

Not with Marcy. With her, it didn't matter if he'd had
her three hours or three minutes before, he wanted her
again. Immediately. He couldn't get enough of her.

Which was part of the reason he was still awake.

His mind was going in circles. She was leaving.
Maybe not tomorrow, but soon. A few days ago he'd
wanted her to stay because the resort couldn't function
without her. Now his need for her had nothing to do
with her job as his manager and everything to do with
wanting her in his bed. Today, tomorrow, three months
from now.

And that made him restless.

He hadn't let anyone in since Courtney. He hadn't
trusted anyone. He hadn't even trusted himself or his
ability to judge character.

The ones on the page, the ones he created, were easy
to read. He knew them inside and out. Even his vil-
lains, sadistic and evil as they were, did only what he
wanted them to. Outside that comfort zone, anything
could happen. And he couldn't manipulate the situation to his preference.

His eyes strayed to Marcy. She'd pulled the covers
up to her nose, her crown of blond hair the only thing
sticking out. Reaching over, he pulled a lock between
his fingers, the silky texture of it a caress.

Even if he wanted her to stay, she was leaving. The
only reason they'd let this happen was that she wasn't
working for him anymore. And after hearing her con-
fession downstairs, he understood now why that was
so important to her.

He fought a surge of pointless anger when he
thought of the bastard who had hurt and used her.

He wasn't going to solve anything lying here, staring at the ceiling. And he wasn't going to sleep. It wouldn't be the first time in his life he'd pulled an all-nighter. Hell, it wouldn't be the first time this week.

Pushing quietly from the bed, he tried not to jostle Marcy. His office was to the right of his bedroom. It was actually bigger, with a better view and several large windows open to the Caribbean Sea. Most people might have made it the master, since the bathroom actually connected to both rooms, but he'd saved the best room for where he spent most of his time.

Sleeping was an annoying necessity. And since he hadn't taken a lover lately, that was the only thing his bed had been used for. Closing the door behind him, he settled into the soft leather chair behind his desk. He reached automatically for the button on his computer, only to remember there wasn't any power.

Today he was firing that crew. He'd fly another one in from Jamaica if he had to. Of course, that meant he'd have to call the ferry back to the island. He wondered briefly if Marcy would take the opportunity to leave, and then decided he'd find some way to convince her to stay. Even if it meant keeping her naked and occupied until the boat was gone.

His lips twitched at the thought. It definitely had potential. He wondered if he could convince her to experiment with handcuffs. Maybe that was taking it a little too far, though.

He was in a much better mood when he pulled out the printed copy of his latest manuscript, lit a candle his decorator had probably intended to be only for show and settled onto the couch. He might not be able to work forward, but he could take the opportunity to go over what he already had.

MARCY WOKE ALONE. She knew it without even opening her eyes. She reached across the bed, the cool sheets telling her she wasn't wrong. Cracking her eyelids open, she rolled her head so she could see the other side of the bed. It barely looked rumpled.

How could he already be awake?

After the day and night they'd had, she'd been so exhausted she'd felt drugged.

Groaning, she pushed herself up out of the warm cocoon of covers, searching for an alarm clock. There wasn't one. What kind of person didn't have a clock beside the bed?

Frowning, she realized who she was talking about. Simon didn't care anything about business hours. He surfaced whenever he wanted to. *Must be nice.*

There was definitely sunlight coming through the window. Judging from the brightness, it was probably late morning. Ten, she guessed, climbing from the bed.

Her brain felt stuffed with cotton. She desperately needed coffee, but without power or water that wasn't going to happen. Marcy found a robe hanging on the back of the bathroom door and wrapped it around herself. It smelled like him. Clean, warm and male. It was soft, well-worn, and she pulled it tighter around her, letting the material hug her body.

Walking into the kitchen, she opened the small refrigerator and settled for caffeine in the form of a warmish coke. Not her first choice, but better than nothing. Leaning her hips back against the counter, she took several slow sips.

The fuzziness began to clear. She frowned, sweeping her gaze across the kitchen. She'd bet it hadn't been used in days. Possibly weeks. She ran a finger over the top of the backsplash and came away with a glob of dust.

She needed to get housekeeping in here stat.

It was a knee-jerk reaction, one she immediately countered. No, that wasn't her job anymore.

Where was he?

She wondered if maybe he'd gone outside. But surely the door closing would have woken her. She wasn't a heavy sleeper normally—the hazard of living where you worked meant you were on call twenty-four hours.

But she'd been so exhausted that maybe she could have missed him leaving.

Since she'd been standing there, she hadn't heard any noise from the rest of the apartment. But before she went tromping across the resort in Simon's bathrobe, she decided to check to make sure.

The door to his office was closed, but she was used to seeing it that way. Although when she thought about it she realized it had been open when they'd come in last night.

She'd long ago gotten out of the habit of knocking on Simon's door. He never answered when she did, choosing to see a knock as more of a suggestion than a request—one he usually ignored.

The familiar exasperation that accompanied her trips up to Simon's office filled her, an ingrained habit two years in the making. But the minute she stepped inside, it disappeared.

He was slumped on the sofa that stretched along the far wall. A pile of papers was stacked haphazardly on the floor beside him, upside down, the blank side up. Another stack fanned out across his chest. They rose and fell in a steady rhythm with his deep, even breaths. So far, none of them had slid off, but she didn't think that could last very much longer.

The sunlight streaming through the windows at the end of the room didn't reach him, probably the only reason the light hadn't woken him. His hair, dry and lighter now, brushed across his forehead, the ends falling to hide one closed eyelid. His face was relaxed. It was a surprise to see, because she'd always thought that was his normal, everyday expression. Only now, when she truly saw him without anything pulling his face taut, did she realize that wasn't true.

It was an act.

When had she begun to realize that? When he'd sprinted down the path to take charge of the chaos? Or maybe when he'd walked into the fire to rescue a man he didn't know. Or perhaps it was the moment he'd touched her and something hot had sizzled down her skin.

Or maybe she'd known it for a very long time and just hadn't wanted to admit it to herself. It was easier to hold him at arm's length when she convinced herself she didn't like the man he was. But she did like him. Maybe too much.

Shaking her head, Marcy realized it didn't matter when. Her opinion of Simon had changed.

But her course of action hadn't. Hopefully in a few weeks she'd be leaving for a new position in the city. It was where she belonged. And all this would end.

She reached for the papers on Simon's chest, easing them softly out from under his folded hand. He was so peaceful. She didn't want to disturb him. He'd been through just as much as she had yesterday and from the looks of things hadn't been able to drop immediately off to sleep as she had.

Snagging the pile on the floor, she walked across to the desk. She meant to scrape them into neat, even stacks and leave them sitting on the top. But something caught her eye and stopped her as she was shuffling the papers together.

At first it was more a realization of what they were—pages and pages of words—than specifics. *What in heaven's name is he doing?* Why would Simon have a document like this? There had to be hundreds of pages between the two stacks.

Sinking into the leather chair that he normally occupied, she cringed when it creaked, and her heartbeat sped up. Why did she suddenly feel like a burglar trespassing on private property?

Frowning, she looked over at Simon, realized he hadn't moved and chastised herself. She wasn't prying. Okay, maybe she was, but she hadn't started off to do it.

Flipping over the pile from the floor, she immediately saw the words *Chapter One* in bold letters halfway down the first page.

It was a book.

Her gaze flew across to Simon. What was he doing with a manuscript? Reading it for a friend, maybe?

She didn't mean to read it. But her eyes started moving across the page, devouring the words as fast as she could. She was only a few in when it hit her. This was a Cooper Simmens book.

How had he gotten hold of it? The story was one she'd never read—and she'd read everything of his— so she could only assume it was the newest book, one not yet released. A spurt of jealousy ran through her.

Logically, she realized she should probably put it down. But she couldn't stop herself. She kept promising herself she'd stop after this scene or at the end of this chapter. But it never happened.

She had no idea how long she sat there, the sun moving in a slow arch behind her. However long it took to read through 120 pages. Because that's where she was when a quietly menacing voice asked, "What do you think you're doing?"

_11_

ANGER, IRRATIONAL AND BLINDING, rolled through Simon. Waking up and finding his manuscript gone was his worst nightmare come to life. Again.

When Courtney had left him he'd been blindsided, confused and upset. But when he'd realized leaving hadn't been enough for her, helplessness, anger and panic had quickly taken precedence. His work was gone. Not just copied, but every single file on his computer erased. His backup hard drive smashed to bits.

Not only had he lost months of work, but he'd also lost every shred of evidence that could be used to prove the manuscript she'd begun shopping was his. It was a new project, something different from the series he'd been working on previously. There were no common characters he could even lay claim to.

His agent and editor had been aware of the project, but he'd convinced them to let him work on it in secret, since it was a departure from his tried-and-true. He hadn't even given them a synopsis they could use to help him. He hadn't trusted his instincts or his talent enough to let anyone see it until it was done. All he had was a contract for an unnamed book that was due. A book he was unable to produce.

He'd been devastated. He'd lost not only the woman he'd thought had loved him, but also months of work. His reputation suffered. His publisher didn't appreciate the upheaval or the media storm that followed. The saying that any publicity is good publicity was a crock.

The betrayal was almost worse the second time around. Although he had no idea why.

Waking up to see Marcy sitting at his desk reading his manuscript had been like a knife to the gut, reopening a wound he'd long thought healed.

Apparently he'd been wrong.

She jerked her head up when he spoke, guilt clearly stamped across every feature of her face.

"I...I..." she sputtered, a hot flush tingeing her throat and face.

He reached across the desk and snatched the paper out of her hand. Breath hissed through her teeth, shock crossing her face. She turned her hand over, and he watched as a thin line of blood welled across her palm.

For a second he felt guilty. Fought against the urge to kiss it and make it better. No, it wasn't his fault she'd gotten a paper cut.

She looked down at it for a second, as if she wasn't exactly sure what to do. Slowly she brought her hand up to her mouth and sucked.

Mumbling around her palm, she said, "What the hell is wrong with you?"

What was wrong with him? "Nothing. Absolutely nothing. Why would anything be wrong when you're sitting in my own damn office violating my trust? Reading my manuscript."

His voice escalated with each word. He heard himself, but couldn't seem to stop the outburst.

"I'm not violating anything, you big idiot. You fell asleep with these—" she picked up the papers and waved them in the air "—spread all over the place. I was just…" Her words trailed off and her eyes went round.

Simon didn't understand what had happened. One minute she'd been yelling at him, fighting verbal jab for verbal jab. The next she was looking at him as if he'd grown a second head.

The heat that had spilled through his body eased, burned out by the explosion of his initial reaction.

"Wait," she said slowly. "This…" She swallowed. "These—" she gestured again to the papers sitting in neat stacks on the desk "—are yours?"

"Yes."

"This book is yours?"

"Yes."

"You wrote it?"

He didn't know how many different ways she could ask the same question. Was she expecting a different answer? "What did you think?"

"That you were reading it for a friend."

Well, hell. That would have been a great cover story if he'd stopped long enough to think about it instead of flying off the handle.

"Ohmygod." She dropped her head into her hands, covering her face. The back of her neck flushed a deep, dark red.

Simon tilted his head sideways, trying to figure out what was going on. Had he woken up in an alternative universe? He looked around his office. Nope, everything looked the same. But Marcy was definitely not acting the same.

"I just slept with Cooper Simmens," she mumbled into her hands.

With a deep breath and a frown, Simon sank back onto the couch behind him. "Don't tell me you're going to turn into a fan girl." He sighed.

Dropping her hands just far enough to reveal her eyes, she speared him with a sharp gaze. "You know me better than that."

Well, he thought he did, but then he'd thought he'd known Courtney, too, so that seemed like a really bad measuring stick. His only answer was a shrug.

"But apparently I don't know anything about you." She groaned, letting her head rest back against his desk chair. Her eyes closed and without opening them she said, "That's what you're always doing in here, isn't it? Writing."

"Obviously."

"Jeez, Simon. You could have told me."

She jumped up from her chair. Simon watched as she paced across his office and ran her fingers through her hair, ruffling the blond strands into a floating cloud around her face. It was incredibly sexy, the agitated way she moved and the intelligence as the wheels in her brain spun.

Settling back, Simon decided to let her work it all out. And while she did, he worked a few things out himself. She hadn't known the manuscript was his until he opened his big mouth. His mind replayed the vision of waking up and finding her sitting behind the desk reading.

The look on her face had been pure absorption. His exclamation had startled her and it had taken several seconds for her to refocus on the world around her. That was a good thing, right?

It was entirely possible his initial reaction had been a little much. Obviously, she wasn't Courtney and hadn't been in the process of stealing everything he'd worked hard to produce. She wouldn't have been sitting in his chair if she had been, would she?

Relief mixed with the awareness that never seemed to leave when Marcy was anywhere nearby. It was a heady combination that was difficult to ignore. Especially with a hard-on throbbing relentlessly against his fly.

She finally stopped pacing, spinning on her heel to face him. It was what he'd been waiting for, her undivided attention.

"I have my reasons for keeping this a secret."

"But you could have told *me*. I was your manager, Simon. You trusted me with sensitive details about the resort, the finances, everything. If you had told me from the first moment it might have changed our entire relationship."

"And we would have ended up in bed together months ago."

"Yes. No." She blinked. "One has nothing to do with the other."

"Oh, I think it does. All those arguments were just a safe outlet for the passion sizzling between us."

"That's not true. I genuinely didn't like you."

"Keep telling yourself that. You wanted me from the moment you stepped onto this island. Why not admit it? I sure as hell wanted you."

Her mouth dropped open. Slowly she shut it.

"Why do you think my actions and attitude pissed you off so much?"

She crossed her arms beneath her breasts, pushing them high and tight against the opening of his robe. The hem trailed higher up her thigh, drawing his attention. He couldn't stop his eyes from trailing up and down her body.

And she noticed, her lips parting softly and the black of her pupils pushing against the bright blue of her eyes.

"Because you're damn frustrating," she said, but her voice had gone soft and airy.

"Oh, absolutely. I didn't know you from Adam when you first got here. I don't trust blindly, Marcy, and wasn't willing to take the risk of bringing you in. Only a handful of people know who I am."

"Zane!" she exclaimed. "He knows, doesn't he? Son of a bitch. He told me there was more to you than I realized, but he wouldn't explain further."

She was quick. It was one of the traits that made her great at her job, but it was also very sexy.

"Yes, Zane and I were frat brothers in college. He knew me before I sold my first manuscript." He also knew all the details surrounding the theft of his manuscript, because he'd consulted his buddy in the CIA to see if there was anything he could do. Or any way he could retrieve the data from his computer.

"By the time I might have considered telling you the truth, you'd already been here for months. I didn't think you'd appreciate learning I hadn't told you the entire truth."

"Oh, so it was better to keep lying to me?"

"Lying is such a nasty little word."

"Then what would you call it?"

Simon shifted uncomfortably against the leather of

the sofa. "Letting you keep your own assumptions. I don't believe I ever told you I wasn't a writer."

She growled, low in her throat. "No, but you let me rail at you like a shrew on more than one occasion when simply explaining why you were preoccupied or busy could have prevented a lot of frustration."

Surging up, Simon grasped Marcy's wrist and pulled her down beside him. She collapsed onto the sofa in a pile of arms and legs, a huff blasting through her lips. She tried to get up, but he tugged again, keeping her there.

He leaned against her body, bringing his lips to her ear. "Maybe I like it when you're a bit of a shrew. It actually turns me on."

Her breath caught in her lungs. But it didn't take her long to start pulling at her wrist again. "You're laughing at me."

"Not on your life. I'm serious. I like it when you get upset. Your skin flushes and your eyes darken and flash." His lips trailed down the soft curve of her neck. Her pulse beat there, steadily increasing beneath the heat of his caress. "It was the closest thing I could get to seeing you go wild in my arms."

"You should have told me, Simon."

"Maybe, but you know now."

She frowned, tilting her head sideways out of his range. She turned, slowly, to look at him. "Not because you told me. You probably never would have if I hadn't found that manuscript on the floor."

Her eyes searched his face. He knew exactly what she was looking for, some sign that he was going to try to lie to her. But he wouldn't do that. At least, not now.

"Probably not. Don't take it personally, Marcy. I don't let anyone in that far. Not anymore."

She brushed a single finger over his lips. Darting out his tongue, he tried to suck it deep inside his mouth. She wouldn't let him, instead pulling back.

"And you aren't going to elaborate on that and tell me why, are you?"

He shook his head, sadness rolling unexpectedly through him.

Simon had no idea what Marcy might have said, what she might have done, because before she could do anything a loud knock echoed through his apartment. Part of him wanted to ignore it, to push her and see where this went. But most of him just wanted out of the conversation before he did or said something he'd regret—like spilling his guts at her feet.

He opened the door to Xavier. Realizing he couldn't ignore the man, Simon swept his arm toward the office door, inviting him in.

Marcy had pulled her bare feet up onto the couch beside her, burying them beneath the edge of his robe. She self-consciously tucked a strand of hair behind her ear, but other than that gave no sign of her discomfort at being caught in his office practically naked.

Xavier didn't pause more than a heartbeat before nodding and saying, "Marcy."

Leaning back against the edge of the desk, he addressed them both. Smart man. Marcy might have told him several times that she wasn't in charge anymore, but Xavier obviously wasn't going to burn any bridges just yet.

"I'm taking everyone off fire rotation. Things look fine and I don't expect any problems. I'll keep an eye on the area from the Crow's Nest, though, just in case. Obviously the shed is a total loss, but we can deal with that later."

Simon nodded.

"We need to talk about the construction crew. They'd like to leave to see to their friend."

"But we have a contract," Marcy protested.

"That I really have no desire to enforce," Simon countered, the right side of his lips twitching upward. She couldn't stop herself. She might not want to step in, but her work ethic was just too strong to resist.

Throwing her hands in the air, she pushed herself up from the sofa. He was certain it wasn't intentional, just a tactic she'd learned over the years to compensate for her stature. The power position was never sitting lower than your opponent. "How are we going to finish the repairs and renovations in time if you fire the only crew we've got? Not to mention now we have debris to clear away. They might not be the best, but surely they can handle the simple jobs while we look for someone else."

He liked the way she used the word *we,* but he knew better than to let it mean anything. "What about their friend?" he asked.

"I'm not an unfeeling bitch, Simon. I'll call the launch myself and have them taken to the hospital right now. Losing one day is better than three or four."

"I never said you were."

She grimaced.

Turning back to Xavier, he said, "Arrange for them to be transported to the main island. Please tell them to concentrate on their friend, that I won't need them back again, but I'll compensate them for the lost time."

Marcy scoffed and turned away.

He ignored her. Xavier, apparently happy with his marching orders, turned to leave. Halfway across the room, he stopped short. He continued to face the door for several seconds, as if considering whether or not to mention whatever he'd just remembered.

Finally he spun slowly on his heel, a move that was definitely military precision.

"Apparently Paul and Christine heard some noises last night."

Simon cut his eyes toward Marcy just in time to see the flush that touched her skin. Clamping onto the inside of his cheek, he fought hard not to grin.

"What kind of noises?"

Xavier's eyes studied him, missing nothing. "Sex noises."

Simon raised a single eyebrow. "Imagine that." The sarcasm wasn't lost on his head of security.

"A shirt and pair of pants were found on the bottom of the pool."

Marcy's spine stiffened. No doubt Xavier had known immediately that the clothes were theirs. He'd seen them wearing those exact items last night in the lobby. However, he was smart enough not to point that out.

Simon forced a noncommittal sound through his throat, afraid if he did more he'd burst out laughing. He shouldn't find her discomfort funny, but he did.

"What would you like me to do with them?"

"Leave them on the pool deck. I'm certain the owners will come back for them eventually."

Simon saw the sharp mirth that lurked deep in Xavier's eyes. "Would you like me to pull up the surveillance footage?"

He had to admit he kinda liked this guy. Xavier had a wicked sense of humor paired with a competency that Simon knew he could trust. He was glad. After Zane had left, he wasn't sure he'd find a head of security he'd feel 100 percent comfortable with.

"No!" Marcy exclaimed.

"Not necessary," Simon said a little more slowly.

Xavier shrugged in acquiescence. "Between the fire and being short staffed, no one was watching last night." He dragged his eyes slowly back to Marcy. "Good thing."

She gave him a tight smile. "Isn't it, though?" she agreed, leveling a daggered glare at Simon's chest. He was definitely going to pay for this.

And something told him he would enjoy every minute of it.

12

SHE'D NEVER BEEN so relieved to see someone leave as she was when Xavier finally walked out the door.

The security system hadn't even entered her mind when Simon had pulled her outside. How could she have forgotten that huge detail? Mortification rolled through her. She'd never been one for public displays of affection. She'd never understood the allure of sex in public places.

At least not until last night. She supposed the fear of being caught might have possibly added a layer of danger to the entire experience. But that was as far as she was going. And while some of their guests seemed to delight in their exhibitionist tendencies, she was not about to join their ranks.

Yes, she realized, the moment Simon had scooped her up into his arms and carried her off with the staff watching, everyone had probably known they were headed for his bed. The heated purpose in his eyes had been hard to miss. But that didn't mean she wanted herself on display.

Sagging against the edge of Simon's desk, she let it take the weight of her embarrassment.

"That was interesting," Simon said from across the room.

"What was?"

"Watching you squirm," he said, sliding in front of her. He wrapped his arms around her waist, pulling her into the cradle of his body.

"I do not squirm."

"Like an inchworm searching for the next leaf."

She rolled her eyes. "How could I not have known you were a writer? Only someone who makes their living using words would say something like that."

His eyes, bright and playful a moment before, became suddenly sharp and serious. "Because you saw what you expected to see. What you wanted to see."

"What you wanted me to see."

"Are we going to cover this ground again?"

She twisted her lips into a crooked line. He had a point. It wouldn't do any good to rehash what was already done. But she wasn't completely ready to let it all go. There was more he wasn't telling her. And that bothered her. She didn't like secrets. Especially her lover's secrets. They'd come back to bite her in the ass before and she really didn't want that to happen again.

"I suppose not. For now. But don't think the conversation is over."

Heat seeped into her skin where his hands spanned her hips. Her body tried to convince her to give in to it, to drag him back to the still-rumpled bed and forget everything else for a little while. But that wasn't going to work. Not right now.

Shoving against him, she slipped out from beneath his arms.

"I'm going to make you a deal."

"Does it involve letting me see what's under my robe?"

"Not right now."

"Then I'm not interested." He reached for her, trying to pull her back to him, but she resisted.

"Oh, I think you will be." She scooted away, putting the desk between them as a barrier. Without it, she didn't trust herself to stay on course. "Why did you need me here?"

His eyes were shrewd as they roamed her face. She watched as he measured the distance across the desk, calculating whether he could reach her before she was out of range.

Rolling the chair in front of her, she added another layer of defense.

"I'm serious, Simon. Why was it so important to keep me here that you canceled the ferry and practically kidnapped me?"

"The book's late and I needed these two weeks to get it finished. If I don't, my editor and agent are going to draw straws to see who gets to murder me."

Jeez, even now he joked.

"And I knew I couldn't handle everything here and finish without you."

Marcy ground her teeth together. Idiotic man. She wanted in on the straw draw, but she'd worry about that later.

"I'm going to ignore that you chose kidnapping me rather than telling me the truth. For now." The flash of guilt that crossed his face was almost enough to make her forgive him. But not quite.

"I will take care of the resort so that you can concentrate on finishing your book—on two conditions."

He looked at her warily but asked, "And what are those?"

"First, you understand that I will be leaving. Soon. I want this job in New York, and even if it doesn't work out the next one will."

She knew he was probably going to have the most trouble with this first one, which was why she'd led with it. And she wasn't wrong. The muscles in his jaw worked as he fought against his initial instinct to argue with her. She had to give him credit for the restraint.

"Fine," he conceded reluctantly. "As long as you leave open the option that you might want to stay."

"Because we slept together?" She tried not to scoff. "Simon, I'm not stupid. You aren't the kind of man who does long-term. And I'm not looking for a relationship."

His face was stony, but he didn't argue. "Second?"

"You can't question any decision I make. If I'm back in charge, I'm back in charge. And now that I know you have other things to concentrate on, I want you to butt out."

Simon rolled his eyes heavenward. "Now she wants me to butt out. I've been telling you for months that I don't care what you do."

"Bullshit. But that's neither here nor there. I promise I'll have power and water back up and running within twenty-four hours."

"All right, but I have a condition of my own."

Marcy eyed him warily. "What is it?"

He shook his head. "Uh-huh. I'm not telling you until you stop acting like I'm an animal about to pounce on you and come out from behind that desk."

Marcy raked her eyes up and down his body. She realized it was probably a trap. But considering he was naked from the waist up, she'd done well to resist him as long as she had.

"Behave," she admonished as she scooted slowly to the right.

He flashed her a smile, full of fake innocence. The minute he could reach her, he wrapped his hands around her body and pulled her against him.

"No going back to the way things were before," he growled against her mouth as he crushed her lips with his. "I don't care if you are working for me again. I need you in my bed. I can't concentrate anymore. All I think about is you."

Her knees went weak. Man, he was good. He knew exactly what to say to devastate her.

"You give me more credit than I deserve," she whispered. "I couldn't resist you to save my soul."

"Thank God for small favors."

His hands roamed restlessly up and down her body. They had no specific destination, touching, caressing, teasing wherever they landed. He pushed his knee between her thighs, pressing them open.

"One more thing," she said, completely breathless from desire.

"Anything."

"Be careful what you promise."

A grunt was his only acknowledgment of her warning.

"I want to read it."

He stilled. And pulled back far enough that she could see his eyes. He was surprised, she realized, and that surprised *her*.

"Why?"

"Because it's damn good. And I want to know how it ends. And because I'm a huge fan."

He laughed, the warm, rich sound rolling through her chest. "Of course you are."

This time she was the one reaching for him, pulling him against her body. She sucked gently at the pulse thudding beneath his jaw.

"Don't let it go to your head."

MARCY SAT IN HER OFFICE. She had to admit it felt good being back behind the desk. She'd handled the problem of the construction crew. The group they usually used would arrive tomorrow. After contacting several plumbers and electricians and explaining the situation, she'd found two who had promised to have the problem fixed within the twenty-four-hour time frame she'd foolishly promised Simon.

They'd exceeded her expectations. The power had been restored the night before. And while part of her had been looking forward to sex with Simon by candle-light, air-conditioning and coffee had been much more important.

And when the plumber had water restored early that morning, Marcy had almost kissed the man's feet. She would never underestimate the importance of a hot shower again in her life. Unfortunately, the reservoir system had been depleted and wouldn't be restored again until it rained, but in the meantime everyone on that system had been moved to vacant hotel rooms.

And considering it was hurricane season, Marcy expected the reservoir to be refilled in no time.

Things were shaping up nicely.

The desk chair creaked as she sank farther back into it. For the first time in a very long time she didn't feel stressed at work. She was…happy. And while it felt a little weird, it was also good.

Looking around her, she realized there wasn't anything else for her to do. She got up and was just about to flip off the light switch and leave for the afternoon when her direct line rang.

Picking it up from the opposite side of her desk, she hoped the call wouldn't take long. She had the sudden urge to spend some serious time on the beach. She wondered if Simon had finished his work for the day and might be persuaded to join her.

"Marcy McKinney, how can I help you?"

"Ms. McKinney, this is Richard Bledsoe from Rock Island Hotels."

She knew perfectly well who he was. "Mr. Bledsoe, wonderful to hear from you."

"I wanted to let you know you're at the top of our list of candidates for the general manager position. Everyone enjoyed speaking with you the other day and we're very excited about your ideas for expanding the hotel and filling our vacant spaces. We were impressed with the marketing campaign you put together for Escape, and the results."

"I'm so glad to hear that." Marcy's heart fluttered uncomfortably inside her chest. She hoped he couldn't hear the pounding tattoo through the phone.

"There are a few people on our hiring committee who raised concerns, since we weren't able to meet with you in person."

Marcy frowned. Damn it!

"However, I think I've convinced them that combined with a letter of recommendation from your current employer, the video conference should suffice as your final interview. If you can provide that for me by the end of the week, I can guarantee the position will be yours."

Euphoria bubbled inside Marcy's chest. Somehow, and she had no idea how, she managed to keep it down. In a calm, professional voice, she said, "I don't think that will be a problem, Mr. Bledsoe. I'll have Simon, um, Mr. Reeves fax it to you as soon as possible."

She took down his fax number, handled the niceties and the minute the phone was on the cradle let out a huge whoop.

"Well, you're certainly happy about something. Can't be our miraculous return to civilization, since that happened this morning."

Marcy whirled around. Simon lounged in her open doorway, his right shoulder pressed against the jamb, his hands shoved haphazardly into his pockets and a wide smile on his face.

It was hard to keep the excited expression from her own face.

"I got it."

The light dimmed just a little in his eyes, but she hardly noticed.

"That was Mr. Bledsoe. He said I got the job. Well, actually what he said was that if you faxed him a letter of recommendation by the end of the week I'd have the job."

She reached for his hands, pulling him along with her as she spun around her office. Everything she'd worked so hard for was falling into place. In a few short weeks she'd be back in New York, in the thick of things, managing a world-renowned hotel.

Her old boss could eat his heart out. Actually, she'd love to be a fly on the wall when he heard she was coming back. And to such a powerful position. No longer someone's lackey, running errands, taking orders, being the scapegoat when things went wrong and getting no credit when everything went right because of her hard work. She was going to be the one in charge.

It took her a few minutes to realize Simon was far from as excited as she was. He moved with her around the room, but only halfheartedly.

She stopped, finally focusing on him. He wasn't happy. But then, she really hadn't expected him to be. The man had kidnapped her rather than let her leave the island. And, yes, she now knew the real impetus behind that move. She had to assume he still wouldn't be thrilled when she left.

"I'm pleased for you. I know this is what you want."

"I'm sorry, Simon. I didn't think. Of course I won't leave you in the lurch."

"I know that, Marcy."

She licked nervously at her lips. "You'll send the letter, right?"

"Of course."

She started to smile, but it just wouldn't form completely on her lips.

"We both knew this wasn't going to last." She moved her hand through the space separating them.

Simon nodded. "Yes, but that doesn't mean I have to be happy about you leaving. I need you, Marcy. I can't finish my book without you here. I don't have time to deal with anyone new right now."

She tried not to be hurt, but it was a difficult thing. Of course his reluctance had nothing to do with her personally or the affair they'd begun. She'd been an idiot to even consider it for the few minutes she had. They'd both been clear from the beginning that it wasn't going anywhere permanent.

It still stung to hear him say her value to him was in

keeping the complications of running the resort from disturbing him.

"You don't have much more, do you?" she asked.

"No. I should be able to finish by the end of next week."

"Well, I promise not to leave before you're done."

"What about Mr. Bledsoe?"

"Surely he'll appreciate integrity in a future employee. I'll just tell him I can't leave you high and dry."

Simon's fingers brushed softly against her cheek. Her first instinct was to lean into the caress, but something stopped her. The ease and comfort they'd found together over the past couple days had been marred by his reaction.

She shouldn't let it bother her, but she couldn't help it.

"Thank you," he said, the corners of his lips lifting for a moment before going flat again.

Shaking his head, he flashed her another smile, but this one didn't go all the way up to his eyes. An ache settled in the center of her chest.

"We need to celebrate. I'll call Chef and ask him to prepare a special meal. Go home, put on something beautiful and meet me in the dining room in an hour. We'll have the place to ourselves."

A shiver snaked down Marcy's spine. A romantic dinner sounded perfect. She knew it wasn't, but she wanted desperately for the special celebratory feeling to be real.

How long had it been since she'd planned that romantic welcome dinner for Lena and Colt, the couple who were supposed to pose for their advertising campaign? At the time she'd been so wrapped up in the details and worried about something going wrong—

which it had—that she hadn't really thought about what she was doing.

Afterward, when everything had fallen apart, Colt refusing to let her use the photographs and threatening to get an injunction against them, she'd looked at the pictures from that night and felt this bone-deep longing for what Lena and Colt had.

Sure, it had taken them longer than it should have to realize they loved each other and belonged together, but their love had been obvious to anyone who'd seen those photographs. She'd definitely recognized it.

Tonight she wanted that. And she wanted it with Simon. The problem was, she knew she shouldn't. Because even if tonight was perfect…it wouldn't be enough.

13

WITH THE POWER FINALLY restored, the restaurant no longer looked like a creepy, deserted building harboring serial killers around every corner. Instead, soft candlelight flickered over the empty tables, glinting off crystal and expensive silverware.

Simon could probably count on one hand the times he'd ventured inside the room. At least, once everything had been set up and the resort opened. After that, he'd left things to the talented chef and maître d' he'd hired. Rarely did he feel the need to sit at a romantic table by himself, especially when the kitchen would deliver to his apartments.

Now Marcy sat across from him and he realized he should have done this much sooner.

Although she probably wouldn't have agreed to it then.

She was beautiful, an intriguing mix of soft and hard. Wispy blond hair curled around her shoulders. The sloping line of her jaw begged him to lean across the table and take a bite of *her* instead of the food sitting in front of him. But the sharp, direct, intense eyes that strayed over to him again and again made a mix of emotions tumble through his body. Awe, desire… and if pressed he'd admit a little bit of fear.

Marcy was a force to be reckoned with. He'd seen her in action plenty of times, and while going toe-to-toe with her always brought on a delicious burst of adrenaline, it also challenged him.

He didn't want her to leave.

And that made this night bittersweet. They were here to celebrate a job offer that would eventually take her away from the resort. Away from him. And the thought made him crazy. He wanted to yell at her, to forbid her to leave, to force her to stay.

And that had worked so well before. Acrid sarcasm curled in the pit of his stomach. He put his fork down on the edge of his plate, unable to eat any more. Chef was not going to be happy.

Simon couldn't ask Marcy to stay. The expression of sheer joy on her face when she'd hung up that phone had punched him in the gut. Leaving was what she wanted. And he'd known that.

Falling in love with her was his fault. His problem to deal with.

The thought formed, at once surprising but also completely easy and somehow right. Of course he loved her. Who wouldn't? She was intelligent, sexy, strong and confident.

In the time they had left, he was going to put on the best game face he could find and pretend a happiness he didn't really feel. The one thing he couldn't handle would be seeing pity in her eyes before she walked away from him.

"The replacement construction crew will be here in

the morning," she said, glancing up at him through the shield of her lashes.

Simon shook his head. "I don't want to talk about the resort, Marcy."

She mimicked his move from earlier and precisely laid her fork on the edge of her plate. He noticed she'd eaten only about half of her food. He was going to have to smooth some ruffled feathers in the kitchen for sure. But that was a problem for later.

Pushing her plate away, she folded her arms on the table in front of her and leaned forward. "Then what do you want to talk about?"

He'd spent the past two years with Marcy. They'd fought. They'd loved. A warm river of desire melted into his blood along with the hope that he'd have her again in a few short hours.

But all he knew about her was what she'd put on her résumé. And what he'd picked up here and there as they'd interacted. He had no idea if she had sisters or brothers or if running a resort had always been her life's goal. He might know what college she graduated from, but not if she'd enjoyed the experience and reveled in the freedom as he had.

And that made him feel a little sheepish. He knew the color her skin turned when she was frustrated, the way her breath caught in her chest when he touched her, the warm sound of her laugh. But he hadn't taken the time to *know* her before he'd set out to seduce her.

And while that had never bothered him in the past— what difference did it make if he knew those kinds of details about a woman he had no intention of seeing again?—he found with Marcy it did. She was so much more to him.

"How did you get into hotel management?" he

asked, settling back into his chair. He needed to put some distance between them so that he could concentrate on her answers.

"My dad," was her succinct answer.

He waited for her to elaborate, and when it became obvious she wasn't going to, he prompted, "And…"

"And he was a hotel manager. My mom died when I was young." He watched as she played absentmindedly with the gold ring on her right finger. "It was just the two of us."

Okay, so no siblings. He could relate.

"With him, life was always an adventure. We lived in big cities with museums and gardens and theaters. Hotels were my playground."

"Like Eloise."

She smiled. "Now, that's something I never would have imagined."

"What?"

"Cooper Simmens, fan of little-girl storybooks."

"Hey, it's all market research. Besides, I have friends with small children."

She laughed, the sound tingling down his spine.

"You're close to your father." It was a statement, not a question. He could see the happiness and connection she had with her father shining from her eyes. "How come he's never been to visit you?"

The brightness dimmed, clouding with a sadness that he wanted to kick himself for causing.

"He died five years ago."

"I'm sorry."

She gave him a slow, sad smile. "Thanks. I try to remember the good times instead of the bad. He was sick for a while at the end."

Simon wanted to see that brightness again, so he asked, "Tell me about one of the good times."

She considered him for several seconds. Her fingers fluttered atop the table, a "thinking" gesture that he'd noticed she had. She couldn't sit still, even when her mind was whirling.

"I think you'll like this one. Dad was always a reader. One of my earliest memories of him involved the two of us cuddling up on the couch before bedtime, Dad reading me a story. As I got older we'd each have our own book.

"I remember the first time I picked up his, wondering what kind of story interested him. I think I was probably twelve or thirteen. I can't even remember what it was now, but I do vividly recall him telling me that it would scare me and that I couldn't read it until I was a little older.

"I pestered him relentlessly until he finally gave in. I don't doubt he started me out on something easy, a psychological thriller that kept me up half the night turning pages. I quickly progressed to Stephen King, which he regretted when it kept me up worrying about evil clowns and rabid dogs.

"Even when I'd made friends and was spreading my wings, Dad and I always came back to reading. It was something we shared."

Simon watched as she reached for her wineglass. She'd barely touched it, but now it seemed to be the most interesting thing in front of her. She ran her fingers up and down the stem, staring into the clear glass instead of at him.

"We read your first book together." She darted a glance at him through her lashes before jerking her gaze back down to the mesmerizing wineglass. "Actu-

ally, I read it out loud to him during his first stay in the
hospital. He was too weak to hold up the book himself
at first."

She laughed and he couldn't help the soft smile that
tugged at his lips.

"Your books got him through three more trips to
the hospital and hospice care." She looked up at him,
unshed tears making her blue eyes glisten. "Thank you
for giving him a little peace."

Simon swallowed. He'd gotten those types of letters
during his career and they always meant something to
him. But this was so much more. This was Marcy sitting in front of him, sharing pieces of her life, telling
him how his work had given her hurting father a few
moments away from the pain.

It was more than he'd expected. And he didn't know
what to say. He used words to make his living and for
the first time in his life couldn't find the right ones.

Dropping her head into her hands, she rubbed at her
eyes for a moment. Her voice was muffled behind the
curtain of her palms, but he heard her anyway. "God,
how depressing. I'm sorry."

"No." He reached for her hand, pulling it away from
her face so that he could see her eyes. "Thank you. I
think that's the best compliment I've ever gotten. I'm
just sad you had to go through that."

Marcy sighed and waved her hands as if to clear the
air of the whole thing. "I had lots of great years with
my dad. We were really close. Not everyone has that.
I'm lucky and I know it. And I wouldn't trade a single
minute of the time we had together. He taught me to
appreciate what I've got, and the best way I can honor
him is by remembering that."

God, she was strong. If he hadn't known it before,

he would after hearing her say that. He admired her for that strength and integrity and wished he could be more like her.

"Enough about me. How's your book coming? Has Francesca figured out who's trying to kill her yet?"

If he'd known talking about his book would be the thing that put fire, excitement and a happy glitter back in her eyes he would have started there rather than making her recall something difficult. They sat in the restaurant for hours, picking at every single dessert on the menu, talking about not just his work but other books they'd both read and loved.

It was something he hadn't done for a very long time, and until that moment Simon hadn't realized how much he'd missed it. The freedom to talk with someone about the story, how it was going, where it was wrong, what questions had cropped up during his creative process… It was exhilarating.

And when she left he'd lose that, too.

Once again he'd be locked alone with his secret. When he'd moved to the island without telling anyone three years ago, it had felt like the right decision. Sitting across from Marcy, he was no longer certain that was the case. He was afraid that without her, it wouldn't be the same.

"Marcy."

The voice startled her and she jerked her head up from the computer screen she'd been staring at for the past few hours. Realizing if she didn't leave Simon's apartments he'd never get any work done, she'd come downstairs to her office. She'd needed to begin the long process of finding him a replacement manager and preparing a detailed accounting of the responsibilities she handled for whomever he ended up hiring.

She tugged self-consciously at the red striped T-shirt she'd grabbed out of her drawer when she'd visited her bungalow this morning. She couldn't believe it had been days since she'd slept there, and that she wasn't missing the sanctuary she'd always found in her small home one single bit. She'd discovered something better—Simon.

For about three seconds she'd tried to talk herself into putting on one of her trademark suits, but that hadn't gone very well. She was on vacation, sort of. The resort had no guests and she was the only person who worked in the front office and was still on the island.

She looked up at Nicole, one of their massage therapists, and tried to work up the guilt she would have felt last week at being caught behind her desk without all her professional armor in place. But it just didn't come.

"What can I do for you?" Marcy smiled at the petite brunette. Marcy had never taken the time to indulge, but guests raved about Nicole's magic fingers.

"Not a thing." Nicole smiled back. "But I can do something for you."

Marcy raised a single brow. "Oh?"

"Simon told me to take you to the massage hut and give you an hour."

She started to protest. "That's very nice, but not necessary. You're on vacation. Simon shouldn't be asking you to work."

"I don't mind. Really, my fingers need a workout or they're going to get lazy. Simon said you'd try to refuse, though, and he told me I couldn't take no for an answer."

Marcy felt a flutter of anger brush through her body. "Well, Simon doesn't get to dictate what I do."

Nicole laughed softly. "He said to tell you he wouldn't let you see what he's been working on if you refused."

Bastard, Marcy thought, but she had to give him credit for the maneuver. The sneaky man knew she was dying to read his latest pages. It was blackmail, pure and simple, but he was, after all, trying to do something nice.

She was making a mountain out of a molehill, but old habits died hard.

"All right," she said reluctantly. "Let me finish up here. I'll meet you at the massage hut in about fifteen minutes, okay?"

"You won't regret it," Nicole promised.

"I'm sure I won't. I have a file almost an inch thick of guest feedback singing your praises."

She shrugged. "I'm good, what can I say?"

Several minutes later, Marcy was heading down the path toward the beach. Massage hut was probably not the best name they could have given the place. Hut didn't do it justice at all. The structure was impressive. Large and round, built high on stilts, it jutted out over the tempting blue depths of the Caribbean Sea.

Deep-colored panels of polished local wood ran around the room, but went only halfway up. The top half of the room was completely open, providing the soothing lap of water against sand and a calming view of the sea. A tall thatched roof rose in the center, the rustle of the straw only adding to the atmosphere of relaxation.

The structure was high enough that no one could look in, so no guests ever felt worried about their modesty. In fact, the beach area for twenty feet in either direction was blocked off so no rowdy beach play could intrude.

Marcy had to admit that she'd always wanted to schedule an appointment, but it just never seemed to happen. She was a little excited as she walked through the open doorway to find Nicole waiting for her. She was fiddling with a line of bottles that ran the length of a low shelf.

"I'm going to step out and let you get undressed," she said, indicating the privacy screen at the far end of the room. "Lie facedown under the blanket and relax. I'll be back in a few."

Marcy tried not to be self-conscious as she folded her clothes into a neat pile. The screen was strategically placed so that she had only three or four steps to the massage table Nicole had indicated. She realized no one could see her, but she couldn't help feeling as if she was doing something naughty by walking naked across a public place in broad daylight.

An unexpected thrill rushed through her, sending goose bumps down her spine. Jerking up the blanket, she dived beneath the soft surface and situated herself. Apparently "sexy rebel" was not one of her characteristics.

Her heartbeat evened out as she took several steadying breaths. When she put her face into the face cradle, a sweet and relaxing smell filled her lungs. Vanilla maybe, although she couldn't be sure. She'd have to remember to ask Nicole. Her eyes closed and after a few moments she realized her lungs had synchronized with the ebb and flow of the water washing beneath them.

The floorboards creaked behind her, but she didn't

turn to look at Nicole as she entered. Instead she asked, "What's that scent. Vanilla?"

A quiet affirmative hum was her only response. Marcy wondered if maybe she wasn't supposed to talk. It wasn't as if she'd ever done this before. Were there rules? Maybe she should have asked that before she got naked.

Nicole's warm hands pressed lightly into the blanket against her back. They rubbed slowly up and down. Marcy inhaled deeply, held her breath and let it out slowly, releasing the tension she hadn't even been aware she was holding inside her body. A low hum of pleasure rolled through her and for a minute she was embarrassed at her reaction.

But Nicole didn't seem to notice or care. After a few moments she felt the soft breeze of sea air against her naked back as the blanket was folded down to her waist. It went lower than she'd expected, stopping just at the top swell of her rear end.

But as soon as Nicole's hands touched her skin she didn't care anymore. Her muscles warmed with a deep heat as insistent fingers dug into her back, worked along her shoulder blades and kneaded her spine. Nicole was stronger than she'd expected. And her hands were larger, spanning halfway across Marcy's back without even trying. Marcy had never really noticed that about the other woman, but maybe that's why she was so damn good.

Thumbs dug into the dip at the base of her spine, rubbing against the abused bundle of nerves that rested there. Another gasp of pleasure and relief leaked through her lips as the muscles on either side pulled tight and then released.

Unexpected fingers of arousal arrowed out from that

spot to settle between her thighs. Marcy tried to tell herself it was a biological reaction. Normal. But she fought against the urge to bring her legs tighter together to find some relief.

Before she had a chance to catch her breath, the blanket was replaced over her back and disappeared around her left leg. A draft gusted up beneath the blanket, touching her exposed sex and making her ache. The edges of the cloth were tucked around her hip, leaving the bottom swell of her ass bare.

Marcy tried to shift around, but a hand at the top of her spine stopped her. This time when the hands touched her, she was aware enough to realize something wasn't right. Calluses ran across the top of each one where fingers met palm. Why would a massage therapist who made her living with her hands let them get in that kind of condition?

Strong fingers worked her calf, moving steadily up to her thigh. She could feel the muscles relax just as those along her back had. But there was more. Her body began to throb, to respond with a need for that hand to go higher.

A gasp blasted through her when the fingers slipped, brushing across the outer folds of her sex. Her body jerked at the caress, silently asking for more.

Marcy wasn't sure exactly when she became aware that Nicole was not the one touching her…not that it mattered. She tried to raise her head to confirm—she was the sort of girl who enjoyed fact-checking—but a solid weight at the nape of her neck prevented her from moving.

"Simon," she warned, although the single word lost all its power, directed toward the wooden floor and muffled by the headrest of the massage table.

He didn't say anything. Suddenly the entire blanket that had been covering her body was yanked away. A shiver rocked her and she tried again. "Simon!"

But he was already running his hands up and down her body, pressing her harder into the soft padding of the table.

He continued to stroke her, mixing what probably should have been relaxing movements with stolen caresses. She tried to close her thighs, to restrict his access to her, but she couldn't keep them that way. A few minutes later she'd find herself squirming against the table, opening again and begging him to touch her where she ached.

His lips pressed against her back and his teeth nipped at the low indent of her spine. Her brain told her the person touching her was Simon, but her eyes hadn't seen him and a single finger of doubt kept trying to creep in.

She was fully aware that he'd done it on purpose. Her senses were heightened. Arousal mixed with adrenaline, driving her higher and making her writhe. Her breasts ached, the tight point of her nipples under constant torture as she rubbed against the cotton-covered table. Heat blasted through her.

And when he finally ran his fingers full tilt up the greedy opening of her sex, she nearly flew apart. "Simon," she said again, but this time there was no reproach, only begging.

The pressure of his hands on her body disappeared. Taking the opportunity, Marcy flipped over onto her back. Simon loomed above her, his eyes hot and heavy as they dragged down her body.

"Simon," she breathed again, part relief and part benediction.

Leaning up onto an elbow, she wrapped her hand in the cotton of his shirt and pulled him down with her. She claimed his mouth as expertly as he'd just played her body.

She just hoped the massage table could hold them both.

14

THE TABLE CREAKED and swayed beneath them. Simon didn't care if it collapsed to the ground. He'd buy a new one and it would be damn well worth every penny.

Touching Marcy had been pure torture. It had been difficult to hold himself back. He let her take control, enjoying the frenzy he'd built inside her.

He relished the way her hands moved restlessly over his body, seeking something she couldn't quite find. When her fingers slid beneath his shirt to run up his back her soft purr of satisfaction made the muscles in his stomach twist.

His cock throbbed painfully. It wouldn't take much to have him exploding. And when he did, he wanted to be deep inside her.

He wanted to ruin her for every man that she'd ever meet once she left him.

Marcy pulled his shirt off over his head and flung it away. He was afraid it might have gone straight out the opening in the wall above her head. At this rate he wasn't going to have any clothes left.

Her nails scraped down the planes of his chest,

flicking his stiff nipples and forcing a hiss through his teeth. She didn't bother taking her time, arrowing straight to the waistband of his shorts. She made quick work of the fly. Simon tried to stop her, to slow her down, but she was a force to be reckoned with.

And he had to admit that he liked it.

Diving her hand into his back pocket, she smiled up at him, sultry and promising when she pulled out a condom. Her eyelids lowered over glittering blue eyes. She pushed his shorts down over his hips. They fell to his knees and stopped there. She moved on, leaving him hobbled.

His foot was a half inch off the floor still trying to get rid of the shorts when she rolled the condom down over his erection. The combination of cool latex and warm hands was thrilling. The thing constricted around him. He could hear his pulse pounding heavy and hard in his own ears, could count each beat in the throbbing erection she fisted.

Marcy's tongue licked across her open lips. She spread her thighs wide and guided him exactly where he wanted to be. With her. Buried deep.

In one swift motion he brought them together, her warmth enveloping him and swelling up through his whole body. Simon grasped her head, silky strands of hair weaving in and out of his fingers. He took her mouth, bringing them together in every way possible. They worked together, hip to hip, breast to chest, mouth to mouth. Pushing, pulling, coaxing, grasping for one second more.

He breathed her in, lavender and vanilla. Sucked her tongue deep into his mouth, taking her in just as she was ensnaring him. The tremors that signaled his release began deep inside his belly. Simon clamped them down, refusing to let go just yet. Even with their lips locked, she panted against him, her body bowing up tight beneath him. He could feel the trembling pulse of her orgasm just on the edge.

He stroked in and out of her, reveling in the feel of their joined bodies.

Something hot and brittle expanded inside his chest. It hurt even as it felt good. A tightness that had his eyes closing and his hands clenching tighter around her so he could be sure she was still there.

Emotion overwhelmed him, something that had never happened before. He gasped, his eyes springing open. He found her, staring deep into him.

They came together, both giving in at the exact same moment. Marcy threw back her head, screaming his name at the top of her lungs. He couldn't find the breath to utter a single sound. Instead, he leaned over and drank the words from her lips, letting them fuel him when nothing else could.

They stayed there wrapped together in a tangle of limbs, shallow breaths and sweat-slicked skin. Her racing heartbeat eventually slowed. The steady drum of it against his chest was the only thing that seemed solid.

After a few minutes she mumbled weakly, "At least we didn't break the table."

The ghost of a laugh tried to roll through his chest, but he just didn't have the energy for the full thing. She got the idea, though, shaking her head in helpless agreement.

Tightening her arms around his body, she brushed her lips across his shoulder and said, "You're going to have to tell me where you learned to do that."

"What? Make you scream?" he asked, a satisfied

smirk on his lips. What could he say? He was a smug son of a bitch.

Marcy smacked at his chest, breathless laughter bursting through her slightly swollen lips. "No. Give massages."

"The same place I learned how to make you scream," he said with a completely straight face.

She pushed against him, but a smile glinted deep in her eyes.

"That was a dirty trick."

"What? Making you scream?"

"No," she said, exasperation mixing with laughter. "Pulling a switcheroo. Do you know for about five minutes I wondered whether I was attracted to Nicole."

"Liar. You knew it was me the minute I touched you."

"Maybe," she admitted reluctantly.

"Besides, I hadn't exactly planned on doing it. I set up the appointment with good intentions."

She scoffed. Simon gazed at her innocently. She raised her brows in a silent challenge.

"Really. I wanted to give you a treat. You've more than earned it."

"Well, isn't that sweet. And about two years late."

Simon tried to ignore the guilt her words induced. "True. But better late than never has always been my motto."

"No joke. Perhaps you should look at changing that. Maybe to something old and Latin. *Carpe diem* usually works for me. Seize the day."

"Have you been paying attention? The only thing I want to seize is you." To demonstrate his point, Simon began kissing up the side of her neck.

She tilted her head, giving him better access, but

offered a halfhearted protest. "You are the most insatiable man I've ever met."

Simon pulled back and looked into her eyes. "Only with you." There was no trace of the humor and comfortable banter that they'd been batting back and forth. He was damn serious and it was suddenly important that she knew that.

He couldn't tell her that he loved her, not when she was leaving. But she should at least know she was different. Unique.

She stared at him for several seconds, her bright blue eyes wide with surprise. An uncomfortable buzz zinged between them. She finally broke it by saying, "You sure do know how to make a girl feel special."

"All morning the only thing I've been able to think about was you down here, naked on this table. Do you know how difficult it is to concentrate with a permanent hard-on?"

"Yes."

Simon shook his head.

"I mean, no. But I know what it's like to be so distracted that if you don't find an outlet for the desire running through you, you're either going to explode or go mad."

A smile on his lips, he reached down and claimed hers in a quick caress. "Yes, that," he said against her mouth. "You're not so bad at making a guy feel sexy and powerful."

"Who said I was talking about you?"

Simon jerked back, ready to break some other man's bones. Until he saw the humor she couldn't hide lurking in her eyes.

"Minx."

Pushing up from the table, he grasped her hand and pulled her with him. With a little nudge toward the privacy screen, he said, "Get dressed."

Glancing over her shoulder, she exaggerated the sway of her hips as she walked away. "I think that's the first time you've ever said that to me."

"How about we try for another. Get dressed so you can find the shirt you threw out of this hut."

Sticking just her head around the screen, she countered, "I don't think so. Consider it payment for the shirt you tore."

"You're never going to let me forget that, are you?"

"Not on your life." She smiled, the expression sharp and wicked as she ducked away.

Raising her voice to be heard around the barrier, she said, "Besides, I'm covered in oil. Do you know how hard it's going to be to get the sand off my skin if I go out on that beach right now?"

He pulled on his shorts and crossed the room. Leaning against the pillar closest to the privacy screen, Simon shoved both hands deep into his pockets and watched as she dressed. Her back was to him, so she didn't realize he was there until he whispered, "Not hard at all, especially if I help."

She whirled around, her shirt pressed against her chest.

"You haven't seen my shower yet, have you?" Simon let his eyes travel slowly down her body. All he could think about was grabbing that shirt from her hands and taking her again. However, he refrained. "It's pretty big. Definitely room enough for two."

They never did find his shirt. When they went back several hours later, it had disappeared, probably taken out to sea with the receding tide.

OVER THE NEXT few days they settled into a routine. The new construction crew had arrived and were working hard to complete the repair list before reopening. Marcy spent most of the day at her desk, handling whatever resort business came up. Simon locked himself inside his office and she tried very hard to make sure no one disturbed him. At night they'd come together. She'd give him a rundown and he'd tell her what he'd written.

Marcy basically moved into his apartment, using the small kitchen there for probably the first time since Simon had renovated the place.

It was easy and scared the shit out of her.

She knew it couldn't last, but the longer she stayed the more she wanted it to. A sense of dread began to turn her stomach at odd times. She was waiting for something to go wrong, for Simon to turn back into the antagonistic, self-absorbed, infuriating man he'd been before. Or for another disaster to befall the hotel.

She'd even taken to checking the National Hurricane Center website several times a day for forecasts. No storm was heading their way…yet…but she just knew the ease and happiness couldn't last.

And she was right.

Late Tuesday afternoon she was sitting in her office, looking at the track of a storm that had just formed off the coast of Africa, when her phone rang. Picking it up absently, she answered, keeping her focus on the chart she was studying. It didn't look as if it was heading for them, but if living in the Caribbean had taught her anything it was that storms could veer at any moment.

"Ms. McKinney."

Mr. Bledsoe's voice got her attention, though. She'd

called this morning to make sure everything was progressing smoothly.

"I was surprised to get your message this morning," he said, confusing her.

"I'm sorry? Why is that?"

"Well, when we didn't receive your letter of recommendation we assumed you'd changed your mind about accepting the position. I really wish you'd called me and told me in person, but I respect your decision."

Marcy propelled herself out of her chair, sending it rolling backward to collide with the wall. "What are you talking about? Of course I still want the job."

Marcy's skin flushed hot with anger and then cold with self-disgust.

Simon hadn't sent her letter. And yes, she was pissed off at him for that. But she hadn't followed up on it, either. She knew what Simon was like—easily distracted. She'd reminded him once on Thursday night and he'd promised her it would be taken care of. She hadn't bothered him again, and hadn't actually thought about it herself until now.

She'd been distracted. By him.

Once again she'd let lust cloud her judgment and ruin her career.

Damn it! She wanted to scream. She wanted to storm through the resort and find Simon so she could yell at him.

A sense of betrayal welled up inside her. Had he really not sent the letter because he was distracted, or because he hadn't wanted her to get the job? She was talking about the man who'd practically kidnapped her to keep her on the island. But that was before she'd known his secret and understood why he needed her here.

She'd promised him she would stay until his book was done.

But maybe that wasn't enough for him.

God, she was an idiot.

Mr. Bledsoe cleared his throat and Marcy realized she'd begun to breathe heavily.

"I'm sorry, Mr. Bledsoe. I was just working through some anger. Apparently my current boss didn't send my letter, if I understand correctly."

"Yes."

"Well, I was under the impression that it had been sent." She fought against the small kernel of guilt buried deep in her chest. This was not her fault. But she wondered if Mr. Bledsoe would want to hire a manager who couldn't follow up on the smallest details.

"Oh, my," he blustered. "Well, that is unfortunate. We've already begun to interview new candidates."

Marcy sucked in a steadying breath and then blew it out in a silent stream, trying to find some calm and get her mind in order.

"Perfect. Perhaps I can be part of that group. I could be on a plane to the States in a matter of hours. I know not interviewing me in person was your selection committee's main concern."

A thoughtful hum drifted out of the receiver. "I couldn't promise you anything, Ms. McKinney. I'm not sure the selection committee will reconsider."

"I'll take whatever chance you can give me."

"Very well, if nothing else, they might be impressed with your tenacious attitude. But you'll need to be here by tomorrow at noon—it's the only appointment time I have left."

She'd paddle a boat to St. Lucia herself if she had

to. "No problem. I'll call you as soon as I arrive in the city."

"I look forward to meeting you in person, then."

They hung up. Marcy stared blindly down at her desk for a moment. Then she sprang into action. After her assurance that she wouldn't leave until his book was finished, Simon had reinstated the ferry service. Turning her wrist, Marcy looked at the slender gold watch her father had given her as a college graduation present. She had exactly one hour and twenty-seven minutes before the ferry arrived and she had a lot to do—make plane and hotel reservations, pack...

What she wouldn't be doing was saying goodbye to Simon.

Not only did the man not deserve the courtesy, but she was afraid the sight of him might make her resolve cave. Right now she was angry with him. But if he touched her...she wasn't sure she'd be able to leave.

And leaving was exactly what she needed to do. She refused to let another man derail her career.

Even if he convinced her to stay, how long would he want her around? He hadn't talked about anything permanent. And when he got tired of her, she'd find herself out on her ass yet again.

No, this was the right thing.

And if leaving without telling him goodbye made her seem catty, then that's what she was.

15

It was late when Simon finally looked up from his computer. He'd been sitting in front of it for ten straight hours, bothering to get up only for coffee and bathroom breaks.

But he was finished. At least with the rough draft. The end was always easier for him, the threads finally coming together in a rush sort of like a snowball rolling downhill.

And he was damn happy with it. He only hoped his agent and editor would be as pleased. Although the one person he really wanted to celebrate with was Marcy. Everyone else could wait until tomorrow.

Getting up from the desk, he listened to the whirr of the printer as it spit out the last fifty pages. He walked over to the windows, placing his hands at the small of his back and leaning into a stretch. His spine popped, a mixture of pleasure and pain as his abused muscles finally relaxed.

When had it gotten so dark? And why wasn't Marcy here? Lately she'd been showing up late in the afternoon. And even if she quietly opened his door to check on him and silently walked back out, he always knew she was home. Her presence registered in the back of his brain.

He'd become accustomed to hearing the soft sounds of her feet as she walked through his apartments. Enjoyed the scent of whatever she was cooking for dinner as it filled the space. Sometimes knowing she was there had been so distracting that he couldn't concentrate and soon joined her, hoping they had time for a quick reunion while something simmered. Other times he'd continued working, the comfort of knowing she was there enough to keep him relaxed and in the story.

Where was she?

Strolling through the hotel, he realized that he actually missed the hustle and bustle of when it was full. While running the place was definitely a distraction, hearing laughter and happy voices did something pleasant for his soul. He liked knowing other people were enjoying the island he'd brought back to life. Sure, there was some pride of ownership in there, too, but who could blame him?

With his book finished—ahead of when he'd expected, thanks to Marcy—he was actually looking forward to a few weeks off once everyone returned. Although it wouldn't be long, because the first book in the series was coming out in three months and his publisher had arranged a five-city tour, ending in New York.

He wondered if he could convince Marcy to go with him, pulling up short when he realized she'd probably already be there at her new job.

A frown was pulling at the edges of his mouth when he stopped at her office. Before he even poked his head through the doorway he knew the office would be empty—there was no light shining through the door. Maybe she'd run to her bungalow to pick up a few things.

Setting out across the resort, he made it there in record time. The flutter of unease that had begun to pick up speed inside his chest diminished when he saw the light shining from her place. Maybe she hadn't wanted to disturb him. She'd known he was close to the end.

Without knocking, he opened the door and went in. The minute he stepped inside he knew it was all wrong. There was definitely no one home. The first time he'd visited, he'd thought there was nothing of her here. He'd been wrong.

The kitchen cupboards stood wide open, bare of the handmade dishes she'd brought with her. Through the open bathroom, he could see the perfect row of bottles was missing. The rug that had been stretched across the floor, curtains, a metal lamp curved into an abstract form—all rolled, folded and stacked together in the corner.

What the hell?

Stalking through, he yanked open the closet door. The rattle of empty hangers was all that greeted him.

Gone, gone, gone.

Without even saying anything.

Anger mixed with pain, a sharp knife that was lodged in the center of his chest. He reached up and rubbed at the spot, hoping it would help. It didn't.

He was about to storm out when a single white envelope propped against the back of the stove caught his eye. His name was scrawled across the surface in neat, precise letters.

His heart plummeted to his toes, knocking against

several organs on the way down and leaving him bruised and battered from the inside.

His hands did not shake as he reached for it. They didn't. He wouldn't let them.

But his knees definitely wavered as he broke the seal and pulled out the single piece of white paper inside. She hadn't even left him a handwritten note, instead typing it out on her computer as if it was nothing more than a resignation.

He walked unsteadily to the sofa and sank onto it. It was either that or sit on the floor in the middle of the kitchen, and he refused to be that pathetic.

Damn it!

Betrayal, a familiar and unpleasant sensation, welled up inside him. How could she leave without saying goodbye? And he wouldn't even think about the promise she'd made to stay until he was finished. It obviously hadn't meant as much to her as he'd thought.

Why did he have to fall for women who were unscrupulous and self-centered?

Even as he thought the words, he knew they weren't true. Marcy was neither of those things. Courtney definitely deserved the label, but not Marcy. Although knowing that didn't ease the sharp pain.

Smoothing the paper out on his knee, Simon read the letter she'd left him. There was no salutation, not even his name, just a few lines. Short, sweet, with no real emotion at all.

Mr. Bledsoe called and said they never received your letter.

Shit! How could he have forgotten to send that? His entire body sagged back against the cushions.

I convinced them to give me another chance to interview in person, since that was their concern. I had to leave immediately to make the appointment. I left a document titled Marcy's Job Description on my computer. My replacement should find it useful.

Marcy

The paper crumpled in his fist. The corners pinched his palm, but he didn't care. What had he done? Obviously he hadn't done what he'd promised her he would.

He'd been preoccupied. Wrapped up in finishing his book and spending every spare second with Marcy, milking every moment he could, knowing she'd be leaving soon.

But he'd thought he'd have time to prepare. That he wouldn't be blindsided when she simply walked away.

And maybe that's exactly what would have happened if he'd followed through, but he hadn't. He'd screwed up, big-time.

But there was something he could do to fix it.

MARCY WAS BLEARY-EYED and sleep deprived when she walked into the corporate offices of Rock Island Hotels. A pleasant receptionist greeted her and directed her back to Mr. Bledsoe's office. She'd expected to be sent to a conference room full of people staring at her across a long, empty table as they drilled her with questions.

Instead, Mr. Bledsoe stood and welcomed her, asking her to sit in the chair opposite his desk. She'd seen him once on the video conference, but she had to admit he was a little more intimidating in person. He was tall—but then wasn't everyone compared to her?—

with broad shoulders, silver-and-black hair and tanned skin that helped camouflage the lines running across his face.

But his smile was genuine and friendly.

"Ms. McKinney, wonderful to finally meet you in person."

"Marcy. Please call me Marcy," she insisted, grasping his offered hand and shaking. "Is the interview delayed?" she asked, looking out into the hallway trying to see who else she might be speaking with.

"No, it's actually been canceled."

Marcy's heart fluttered uncomfortably in her chest. "I'm sorry. I don't understand."

Mr. Bledsoe sank back into his chair. Marcy followed his lead and did the same. He studied her for several seconds, his eyes quick and intelligent. Marcy shifted nervously under the scrutiny.

"I had an interesting phone call this morning at six o'clock."

"Oh," she said, feigning interest. What did an early call have to do with her and her interview, or lack thereof?

"It seems Mr. Reeves takes full responsibility for not sending your letter. And while I have to admit to some concern that my potential manager wouldn't follow up on such an important detail, he assured me that you were under the impression it had been sent."

"I'm sorry, that's not—" Marcy tried to correct the lie that Simon had obviously told Mr. Bledsoe. All the while, her brain spun faster and faster with the realization that Simon had called this man at the crack of dawn.

Mr. Bledsoe waved his hand as if he already knew what she was going to say and didn't care. "I'm quite impressed with the level of support and loyalty you seem to have earned from your last employer. Mr. Reeves went so far as to intimate he might have not sent the letter on purpose in a misguided attempt to keep you in your current position."

"No, Simon would never do something like that. He's absentminded and gets distracted easily, but he has good reason for that."

He raised a single eyebrow and asked, "Oh?"

Marcy felt a flush move up her skin, but she refused to acknowledge it. Or elaborate. She'd already gotten close enough to Simon's secret and no matter what else might have happened between them, she wasn't about to betray that trust.

It was her turn to dismiss an entire topic of conversation with the flick of her wrist. "It doesn't matter. Simon didn't do it on purpose and you're right, I should have followed up."

Reaching down, she gathered the straps of the briefcase she'd brought with her and started to stand up. "I wish you had called to tell me I was no longer being considered for the position before I came all the way down here, but I suppose I understand your reasoning. I appreciate you explaining to me in person."

She was half in and half out of her chair when Mr. Bledsoe's words stopped her. "You're right, you aren't being considered for the position. It's already yours. I canceled all the other interviews first thing this morning. I'm assuming you'll need a few days to settle in, but I hope you can start next Monday."

Marcy collapsed back into the chair, not caring that her posture was hardly ladylike or professional.

She stared at Mr. Bledsoe, trying to make the wheels

in her brain turn again so she could process what he'd just said.

"I have the job?"

He smiled. "You have the job."

She didn't know what to say. She should be filled with excitement.

But she wasn't.

Sure, she was looking forward to the challenge, to moving back to the city of her heart.

But there was something missing.

"You don't appear pleased," Mr. Bledsoe said in a soft, worried voice.

"No, no, I am. A little shocked is all. And terribly jet-lagged. It was a long trip."

Marcy gathered her wits and managed to have a coherent, relatively professional conversation about the details of her new position. An hour later, she was walking back out the door. This time when she left the receptionist addressed her by name. "Welcome aboard, Ms. McKinney. We're all looking forward to working with you."

Marcy sent her a smile, but she knew it didn't come anywhere close to being real.

MARCY HIT THE GROUND running. Finding a new apartment, settling into a new job... Before she knew it several months had passed. And while she was certainly busy, it wasn't exactly what she'd expected.

Running the flagship hotel for the entire Rock Island Corporation was definitely challenging. And she enjoyed the moments that tested her skills and kept her on her toes.

The job wasn't the problem. It was the hours afterward. She'd lived on her own for almost twelve years. Being alone had never bothered her. But it did now.

She missed Simon. And the resort.

More than she ever would have thought possible.

Considering she'd never really gotten attached to any particular place growing up, feeling homesick was a new experience for her. One she really didn't know how to handle. And the bone-deep loss that accompanied it didn't help.

It had probably taken her two weeks to realize why she was so upset. She'd let herself do the unthinkable and fall in love with Simon.

God, she was an idiot. The problem was she didn't know what to do about it.

She couldn't go back, not after the way she'd left. Simon would never forgive her. Besides, she might love him but she was still a little pissed off at him. True, he'd fixed the problem, but the reality was he'd made her a promise and hadn't followed through.

Although she had to admit, if he were standing in front of her right now, she'd probably forget all that and leap into his arms.

But the main issue was still there. What would she do if she went back to Île du Coeur? She refused to work for Simon while they were lovers. She'd been there before and she wouldn't do it again. Relationships were hard enough without throwing in business to complicate things.

And even if she didn't have a personal history to draw from, her experiences with Simon would have been enough to make her hesitate. The last couple of weeks they'd been together might have been fairly smooth, but she had no doubt that, given time, their tempers, strong personalities and different views on how to run the resort, would have clashed again.

Her choices were to have Simon and lose her job—a huge chunk of her identity—or to lose Simon and keep her job. She respected herself and her business abilities and refused to sacrifice a job she enjoyed and was good at. Especially for a relationship that wasn't a sure thing.

Who knew if Simon would even be interested in picking up where they'd left off? Not once had he given her any indication that he wanted more than the short time she had left on the island.

All of these arguments and insecurities combined to keep her tied to her job in New York, despite feeling unhappy and dissatisfied.

A few weeks turned into three months and as winter set in with a vengeance, she couldn't help but miss the welcoming heat of the island. Before she realized what she was doing, Marcy found herself searching websites hoping to find another Caribbean resort in need of a general manager.

When had her idea of the perfect life changed so much?

She knew the answer to that, but couldn't bring herself to admit it.

16

THE SECOND SIMON WALKED out of La Guardia he missed his island. Not only was New York cold as hell, it was also crowded, dirty, loud and almost made him claustrophobic.

However, the fact that his heart was pounding hard in his chest had nothing to do with this new aversion to crushing crowds and everything to do with the fear that Marcy wouldn't show up.

He was in town for the last stop of a whirlwind book tour. He'd started in L.A., continued through Chicago, Dallas and Atlanta. Being in a different city every day was wearing on him big-time.

But it was almost over. In a couple more days he'd be back home, on the soft sand beaches of his island. It was hard not to hope that Marcy would be standing there with him, but he just didn't know. It had been three months since she'd walked away. He hoped a little space might have given her enough time to forgive him. Or at least made her willing to listen as he groveled and begged her to come back.

Of course, that assumed she'd actually accept the invitation to attend his book signing. He'd had a copy of the book hand delivered by courier two weeks earlier, so he knew she'd received it, the information about the signing and his handwritten note asking her to come.

If she didn't, that would tell him everything he needed to know. Which, if he was honest, just meant he'd have to hustle up her home address and track her down there. He wanted her to come to him on her own terms because that's what she deserved. But, at the very least, he wouldn't leave the city without apologizing to her and telling her that he loved her and wanted her in his life. On whatever terms she dictated.

A car deposited him in front of the bookstore. The crowd that waited for him no longer surprised him. Apparently the rumors from several years ago had done nothing but increase his notoriety. Thanks to his fading from the spotlight and recent reclusive tendencies, his first appearance in years had become something of a media frenzy—at least, that was his agent's take on things. Personally, he just figured this tour had coincided with a slow media week. Everywhere.

He'd always been successful—enough to buy a Caribbean island, for heaven's sake—but this was more attention than he'd ever had before.

His publisher was certainly happy, and he knew the marketing team had been quick to spin the story to the best advantage. He didn't care. Whatever sold books.

He just hoped the crush of people didn't deter Marcy. His eyes scanned the group staring back at him. It took him less than thirty seconds to realize she wasn't there. Even with her short stature, he would have known.

Trying to hide a frown, Simon sat down at the table the store had set up. Stacks of books sat on either side of him. But he'd agreed to a short reading followed by a question-and-answer session before he started signing books. And after four of these things, he already knew what everyone was going to ask him.

And he wasn't wrong.

Eventually they'd get around to their curiosity about his career, this book. Some hard-core fan would probably even ask about the rumors and scandal from three years ago.

But first, they all wanted to know "Who's Marcy?"

"Is she with you?"

"Where did you meet?"

Yeah, the dedication he'd written had gotten even more fan attention than his past, his secrecy and the book itself combined. He tried not to let that bother him, considering he'd also written the dedication. Although that hadn't been for them, but for her.

Who would have guessed people would care so much?

He was about to give the standard answer he'd developed after being blindsided by these same questions in L.A.

But the words died on his lips when someone in the back shifted and he saw her standing there. Her blond hair was pulled back into the same tight ponytail she'd always worn before their precious two weeks. Her cheeks were pink from the cold. A scarf was wrapped around her neck, the ends tucked beneath the heavy folds of her winter coat.

She was thinner, the bones of her face pushing slightly against her taut, chilly skin. She stared at him, her teeth worrying her bottom lip. He wanted to reach out to her, but a crowd of people stood between them.

Her eyes were hesitant. They watched him almost

warily, as if she was ready to sprint away at the first sign of…something. Her mouth stayed straight, unsmiling, although she did raise a single hand in a sort of pseudo wave.

The crowd began to turn to see what had caught his attention and struck him mute. First one, then five and before he knew it hundreds of heads had swiveled to focus on Marcy. He hadn't thought her skin could get any pinker—but he'd been wrong.

But she didn't back down, not his Marcy. Instead, she stared at them all, raising a single eyebrow and daring them to say anything to her. Jeez, she was something to watch.

Clearing his throat, he stood and gestured for her to come up with him. She shook her head. Simon narrowed his eyes and, with nothing more than a cock of his head, challenged her. They didn't need words for him to tell her that she had two choices—come up with him or be mobbed by the crowd between them when he finally opened his mouth and told them who she was.

She might not have fully understood, but she got enough of the gist that she began pushing through the people, trying to find the path of least resistance. Which wasn't hard, considering that they all parted to let her pass.

Everyone in the room realized there was an undercurrent flowing between them, and they all wanted front-row seats to watch it play out.

Marcy halted in front of him. He tried to reach across the table and draw her around to his side, but she sidestepped out of range. His heart did a little stutter. He had to admit the minute he'd seen her standing back there, he'd assumed everything was going to be okay. Why else would she be there?

Especially if she'd read the dedication.

But maybe she just wanted to hear the words. Wanted him to grovel in person.

And he was willing to do that. With an audience, no less.

Marcy was worth it.

Shrugging, he turned to the crowd and said, "This is Marcy."

The deafening roar that went up nearly shattered his eardrums.

The crowd surged forward. Panic and surprise shot across Marcy's face. Several people from the store and Simon's team jumped in front of Marcy to protect her from the people now yelling questions at her.

In the confusion, he reached around, grasped her beneath the arms and bodily pulled her to the other side of the table with him. At least it offered a little barrier.

He wrapped her in his arms, pressing her against him. Everything came flooding back, overwhelming him. He'd forgotten how fragile and perfect she was, and how unbelievably arousing it felt to have her in his arms. The scent of lavender washed over him and he drew a heavy breath just so he could hold it inside him again.

She didn't fight him, but melted against him as she always had.

"What just happened?" She looked up at him with dazed eyes. He wanted to crush his mouth to hers, but realized it probably wasn't the right time.

But it was touch and go there for a minute. Three months had never felt so long in his entire life.

"You started a moment of hysteria."

She blinked slowly. "How did I do that?"

"Just by being you."

She nodded as if she understood, but he could still see the confusion in her eyes. "That makes no sense."

He shrugged. "What can I say? They like the dedication."

Her bright blue eyes stared up at him. Around them people peppered them with questions. He heard the words, but let them bounce off him.

"What dedication?"

"You didn't read it? You didn't read the book I sent?"

Slowly she shook her head again. Guilt, pain and something he seriously prayed was hope flitted across her face. She licked her lips and then said quietly, "It hurt too much. I couldn't read it without thinking about us."

Something thick and heavy churned in the pit of his stomach. And yet, despite it, he knew exactly what he had to do.

He let out a loud whistle, and was amazed how quickly the crowd fell silent. Every single eye in the place focused on him, including Marcy's.

Reluctantly he let her go to reach for one of the books stacked high on the table. Facing the crowd, he said, "She hasn't read the dedication." Soft murmurs rippled through the group, but everyone quickly became silent. They all knew what he was about to do. Everyone except Marcy.

She stood there staring at him as if he'd just grown feathers.

Turning to face her, he opened the book and flipped over the first several pages.

"First, I want you to know how many hoops I had to jump through to get my publisher to change this at the last minute. I think I owe them my firstborn child."

A soft twitter from the crowd sounded beside them.

His eyes dropped to the page, but they didn't stay there long. He didn't need to read the words to know what it said. He had them memorized, had agonized over just what he should and could say to her. He didn't want to see ink on paper.

He wanted to watch her. To see the expression in her eyes.

"'Marcy, I might have been able to write this book without you, but it wouldn't have been worth the effort. Nothing matters without you in my life. I know I don't deserve a second chance, but I'm hoping you'll give me one anyway. I love you.'"

Every woman in the crowd sighed in unison. Every woman except the only one who mattered—Marcy.

She just stared at him, her eyes wide.

"Say something," he whispered, although everyone in the place could hear, since they were all holding their breath.

"I love you, too," she said, her voice scratchy.

Another loud roar filled the room, covering up Marcy's next words. "But how are we going to make this work? Simon, you lied to me, broke promises, didn't trust me enough to let me in. I can't go back to the resort and work for you—I refuse to mix business and pleasure. And I won't play Russian roulette with my career again. It's too important and I'm too good."

"I trust you now. With my life. My heart. The resort. Whatever you want. Everything I have, everything I am is yours, Marcy. I promise never to lie to you again. And while I can't promise never to get wrapped up in my head and forget something again, I can promise you I'll try."

Simon glanced quickly at the rapt faces of the audience, realizing he was about to spill his secret to them and the reporters loitering at the back of the room. But if it meant convincing Marcy to come home it would be so worth it.

"Someone I once cared about betrayed me in the worst possible way."

The crowd murmured darkly, knowing exactly what he was talking about.

"My fiancé. After that it was just easier to shut everyone out. To cut myself off from everyone and everything. To hide."

He would have gone on, giving her as many details as she needed, but she stopped him. With a single finger to his lips, she said, "You don't have to explain. I understand."

Of course she did. She'd experienced the same kind of betrayal.

"That doesn't fix our employee, boss, lover problem, though, Si— Cooper."

"I trust you. Now, my question is do you trust me?"

Marcy closed her eyes for several seconds. He knew this was hard for her. She was such a strong, independent person. Putting her faith and future in someone else's hands was difficult. But he really needed to know if she would do that for him.

He'd learned over the past few months that trust had to run both ways. Looking back on his relationship with Courtney, he could admit that he'd known there was something wrong with it, something missing. It hadn't bothered him, though. The sex had been good. She'd been a beautiful hostess and trophy he could show off, along with his expensive apartment and career accolades.

But they hadn't loved each other and had never put

the other first. Not the way they should have if they'd really cared about one another.

The way he cared about Marcy.

Given her history, he understood her hesitation. And, yes, time would prove to her that her fears were unfounded. He had no intention of ever letting her go again, but he also understood her need to work, to feel that she was using her skills. There was a part of her that would always judge her own value by the job she could do.

And her drive was one of the reasons he loved her.

"Absolutely."

"Well then, leave everything to me," he said with a smile. Then he bent her backward over his arm and kissed them both senseless.

17

Simon's hands spread wide over her face, blocking her eyes. Marcy could hear the sound of the waves as they washed against the sand. A soft breeze carried music and laughter.

She'd been back on the island for less than a week and already it was hard to remember the months she'd been gone. They seemed more like a cold dream than reality.

Mr. Bledsoe hadn't exactly been thrilled when she'd told him she was leaving. But she'd stayed on for a month—a lonely month, considering Simon had returned to Escape—to assist in the transition.

A few things had changed in the four months she'd been gone. For one, someone else now occupied her old office. At first she'd been surprised to learn that Simon didn't intend to let the new manager go. Although, considering she'd told him she couldn't work for him, she shouldn't have been. It was just difficult to stand by while someone else did her job. Or what used to be her job.

But once again, he'd asked if she trusted him. He'd

told her a few things were taking longer than he'd anticipated and that she'd just have to wait a couple more days to find out his solution to the entire problem.

Apparently she was going to find out now. Although what it had to do with walking her outside blindfolded, Marcy didn't know.

"If this is just an excuse to get your hands on me, you realize it isn't necessary," Marcy said.

She thought she heard a sound, almost like smothered laughter.

"Trust me, I have every intention of touching you plenty later," he whispered into her ear. His breath tickled, sending a shiver of anticipation racing down her spine.

The new manager had also taken over her bungalow, but Marcy hadn't minded moving into Simon's apartments. After being separated from him for so long, she really hadn't wanted to be anywhere but in his bed anyway.

And they'd definitely made up for lost time. In fact, she'd barely had a chance to be bored or worried in the past week. He'd kept her too occupied—either aroused or exhausted.

"Where are you taking me?" she asked, trying to concentrate on something other than the desire lashing through her. She had to admit, with his hands over her face, the scent of him was filling her lungs and making concentration extremely difficult.

"Almost there. Just a few more steps."

Small sounds began to filter into her brain. The soft shuffle of shoes against concrete. The low hum of whispered voices. Someone saying rather loudly, "Shhhh."

Before she could ask Simon again what was going

on, he dropped his hands from her face to settle softly on her shoulders. Most of the staff stood in front of her, crowded around the garden Simon had built beside the main hotel building to hide the scars from the fire.

He'd done a great job, and she wished she could have seen him in action. From what she'd heard, he'd planted some of the bushes and flowers with his own hands. Now, that she would have paid money to see— Simon with his arms elbow-deep in dirt.

Looking at him now, with his ruffled golden hair, a bright blue Hawaiian shirt that matched his eyes and a deep tan across his skin, he didn't look like the kind of guy who believed in manual labor.

But then, it had taken her more than two years to figure out that the image he showed the world was not a true reflection of the man beneath the surface.

"What is going on?" She turned to look at Simon, her eyes widening. "Who's running the resort?"

"Don't worry. Enough of the staff stayed at their posts. The guests won't even notice the difference."

Marcy hummed deep in her throat, but it was no longer her job to direct the staff. A sharp pain lanced through her chest, but she ignored it. She'd told Simon she trusted him, and she did.

"Okay, anyone want to tell me what's going on?"

"I thought the staff should meet the new owner of Escape."

Marcy just shook her head. "Simon, don't you think you should have done this a long time ago?"

"I did. I wasn't talking about me."

She was confused. Seriously. "What *are* you talking about?"

Xavier handed Simon a sheaf of papers bound in a blue cover. She'd seen enough legal documents to realize they were important, whatever they were. Reaching down, Simon pulled up her hand and set the papers against her palm.

"These documents detail the transfer of ownership for the resort, from me to you."

Marcy blinked at him, certain she'd heard him wrong.

"Excuse me?"

"You own Escape."

Her fingers curled around the pages in her hand. In the back of her mind she heard the rustling sound as the top few crumpled, but somewhere between her brain and hand the signal to relax got lost.

"No." She shook her head. "This is too much."

She tried to grab Simon's hand so that she could shove the papers back at him. Panic and disbelief mixed heavily inside her chest. What had he done?

Simon clasped his hands behind his back. That didn't stop her. She smacked the bundle against his chest, her fingers splayed wide, and held them there.

"It isn't too much, Marcy. This place belongs to you. You care about it. And you're good at running it, unlike me."

"You handled it all just fine while I was gone."

"Maybe," he conceded, but that was as far as he was going.

"But…but…" she sputtered. "What happens if we break up? If you get pissed at me or I get pissed at you or the entire thing falls apart?"

He smiled at her, that charming, mischievous, wicked smile that had always driven her crazy. And it still did, but it also made her heart flutter inside her chest.

"First, I fully expect that both of us will get angry at

some point. We'll yell. Disagree. And then we'll make up. That doesn't mean either of us is going anywhere. Second, I have no intention of ever letting you off this island again."

"Simon," she said in a warning tone.

"I kidnapped you once, do you think I won't do it again?"

His arms came out from behind his back, but instead of taking the papers, he wrapped them around her and pulled her tight against him. Uncaring that the legal documents governing his entire resort were now crushed between their bodies and getting more destroyed by the second.

He wrapped his hands around the nape of her neck, angling her head so that he could stare down into her face. Gone was the playful glint that always seemed to lurk in the back of his tempting blue eyes. In its place, she saw sincerity, love and an intensity that had her bones melting.

"Everything I have is yours, Marcy, because none of it is worth a damn without you. I know this is important to you. You gave up your dream to come back to Escape with me. And I want to show you how much that sacrifice means to me."

Guilt suffused her. "Actually, leaving New York wasn't hard at all." She pressed her forehead to his, bringing them closer together. "I forgot how cold it is there."

The staff laughed and Simon's lips quirked into a smile.

"But mostly, you weren't there. My dream doesn't matter to me anymore if you're not there to share it with."

"So now we're both happy," Simon said. "Besides,

this way I don't have to deal with the headaches anymore. The resort is yours." He raised his head from
hers and turned to look at the people beaming back at
them. "You hear that? Problems go to Marcy. I don't
want to hear about anything. Not even the thread
counts on the sheets."

Marcy smacked at him. "Now I understand. This
was all an elaborate scheme to get out of working. I
should have known."

This time his little-boy smile couldn't hide the hint
of guilt that lurked in his eyes. "Hey, think of it as ef-
fective management. I know my own shortcomings
and I'd be an idiot not to take advantage of your skills.
You're so damn good at running this place."

"Flattery will get you everywhere," she said, her
heart swelling inside her chest.

Before she knew what was going on, Simon was
slipping out of her arms. At first she thought something was wrong, since he was heading for the ground.
But the startled expression on her face didn't last long
when she realized he hadn't fallen over, just dropped
onto one knee.

"Oh, my god," she breathed out. "What are you
doing?" That seemed to be her favorite phrase today.

"I'd think that was obvious," Simon said, mock
frowning up at her from his position at her feet. She
tried to pull him up off the ground, but he wouldn't
budge.

"Marcy, I told the entire world that I loved you in
the most public way I could think of because I want
everyone to know how I feel about you."

A hard lump formed in Marcy's throat and her eyes
glazed over with tears.

Who would have thought almost two and a half

years ago when she'd walked onto this island that she'd end up here with Simon Reeves kneeling in the dirt, about to propose to her? Definitely not her. She'd come here looking for an escape. An opportunity to prove her worth—to herself and the world.

And instead she'd found all of that and more. A man she loved who loved her in return. The kind of person she could see spending the rest of her life with, having children, growing old.

Maybe there was more to that little legend about the island than any of them had ever realized. She'd certainly found her heart's desire and it was nothing like what she'd expected.

"But I wanted to share this moment with the people who've come to mean something to us both," Simon continued. "Some people think of this place as paradise. Some might see it as isolated. But I just see it as home and I want you to stay here with me forever. To build a life together."

"Yes," she whispered, the tears she was desperately trying not to shed choking off the word. "Yes," she said again, stronger and more sure.

A happy whoop from the crowd accompanied her answer.

Simon picked her up and spun her around, bringing their mouths together. The familiar heat spilled into her body, the buzz of it delicious and comforting.

They were definitely going to have some fun adventures together. With Simon, there was no telling what was coming around the corner.

A breathless laugh burst from her body. She was dizzy with happiness. Finally Simon put her down, the world still spinning gently around her.

She gazed unsteadily at the people gathered around them. Friends…no, family.

Marcy wanted every single person who visited Île du Coeur to find the same happiness she had found.

Colt and Lena, Zane and Elle, she and Simon… Marcy really hoped they were part of a long line of couples who would find love here. Which gave her an idea.…

"Simon, I'm going to hire a wedding planner."

"Fine." He shrugged. "I would have expected you to be too ana—" Marcy's glare had Simon choking back his words. "Um…organized…to want to let that go."

"Not for us. For the resort."

Simon's eyes went wide with fear before he apparently remembered that whatever she was planning, it was no longer his worry. "Whatever makes you happy."

Marcy had visions of sunset ceremonies on the beach and grand parties in the ballroom. It would be perfect.

Reaching up on tiptoe, she wrapped her arms around Simon and pulled his mouth down to hers, whispering against his warm lips, "*You* make me happy."

Simon swept her up into his arms again and carried her away, completely uncaring that he was leaving behind the crowd of people who'd come to congratulate them. She'd apologize later. His mouth nuzzled at her neck. *Much later.* The corner of his lips curled in a smile full of devilment and charm and his eyes flashed with heat as he mock growled, "Happy's good. But naked's so much better."

* * * * *

A sneaky peek at next month...

Blaze®

SCORCHING HOT, SEXY READS

My wish list for next month's titles...

In stores from 15th June 2012:

❏ Not Just Friends – Kate Hoffmann

& Coming Up for Air – Karen Foley

❏ Northern Fires – Jennifer LaBrecque

& Bringing Home a Bachelor – Karen Kendall

Available at WHSmith, Tesco, Asda, Eason, Amazon and Apple

Just can't wait?

Special Offers

Every month we put together collections and longer reads written by your favourite authors.

Here are some of next month's highlights—and don't miss our fabulous discount online!

On sale 15th June   On sale 15th June   On sale 6th July

The World of Mills & Boon®

There's a Mills & Boon® series that's perfect for you. We publish ten series and with new titles every month, you never have to wait long for your favourite to come along.

Blaze.® — Scorching hot, sexy reads

By Request — Relive the romance with the best of the best

Cherish™ — Romance to melt the heart every time

Desire™ — Passionate and dramatic love stories